DEATH IN THE TREES

Death in the Trees

A Patrick Dawlish Mystery

John Creasey *writing as* Gordon Ashe

OPEN ROAD

INTEGRATED MEDIA
NEW YORK

Copyright © 1954 by John Creasey

ISBN: 978-1-5040-9814-4

This edition published in 2025 by Open Road Integrated Media, Inc.
180 Maiden Lane
New York, NY 10038
www.openroadmedia.com

DEATH IN THE TREES

CHAPTER I

THE BODY

Dawlish was alone in the room with the dead man. He heard no sound but his own breathing. He saw only the big, white, flabby face, the lock of black hair falling over the forehead, touching one big, protuberant eye.

The bullet, which had entered the right temple, had made little mess. In the centre of the wound was a dark dot, about it a red swelling, beneath it and dripping to the back of the chair, a tiny rivulet of blood.

Behind Dawlish was the open window; the window through which he had entered. The Professor, whom he had come to see, could not have welcomed him. It was a shock to Dawlish to discover that the fat man would never welcome anyone again. It was an acute disappointment, too.

At least three silent minutes passed before Dawlish recovered from the shock and could begin to think.

He moved from the chair and the gross bulk of the dead man's body.

The sight of death did not trouble him. The death of Professor Haffmeyer would, in normal times, have given him cause for rejoicing. Many would rejoice when they discovered it, for he was a traitor to his country. Dawlish had started, long before, to find out why, and to whom he sold his secrets. It had been said of Dawlish that he would travel to the ends of the earth to get what he wanted.

There was more. Dawlish had served his country, through its Secret Service, loyally and well. Now, he was also branded traitor; and Haffmeyer had branded him.

Dawlish wanted to know why; believed he could have made the man talk. But now a man he had cause to hate was dead of violence.

Dawlish looked on the floor.

There was no gun.

He went forward, slowly, and shook his head. That was almost as if he were saying that he knew, in advance, that there was no point in what he was about to do. But he did it. He searched Haffmeyer's pockets. He transferred several papers to his own pocket, but did not find what he wanted—the address of another man.

His thoughts were not concentrated on the immediate task.

He was in a strange country on a mission to clear himself of the charge of treason. They were simple words which meant much more than they seemed to. For him, they meant that he was now in a dangerous country on a deadly mission. The fate of Haffmeyer proved the deadliness, if ever it had been in doubt—for hadn't Haffmeyer been killed to make sure that he would never talk to him, Patrick Dawlish?

Dawlish moved away from the chair and the dead man.

This was a study, on the ground floor of a two-storey house. It was a long, narrow, book-lined room, with white paint, rich colouring of reds and blues in the furniture, the curtains and the square of carpet on the polished pine floor.

Outside was the quiet of the forest.

Three miles away, traffic swarmed and whined along Washington's Highway 99. Police in cars and police on motorcycles merged with the traffic. Once warning was given, they would swing off that broad highway and their sirens would scream as they twisted and turned along this narrow road with its dirt surface. They would fling themselves from their machines or out of their cars, in a few minutes—seconds?—the house would be surrounded.

There might be headlines;

ENGLISHMAN HELD FOR HAFFMEYER SLAYING

There would probably be that and a great deal more, if he were caught.

No one in England and no one here would help him. He knew all the risks, had known them before he had started on this quest.

He finished with Haffmeyer's pockets, and turned towards the desk, in a corner. It was closed but not locked. Nothing in Haffmeyer's possession had suggested that he had been searched; and everything in the desk seemed to be in order.

Dawlish searched the room, until the only place left was the safe. Since the keys were there, it was easy to open it; everything was easy, much too easy. He glanced at the open window and the distant stars; at the silent door. As he looked through the contents of the safe, he was continually alert. It was as if some warning bell were ringing in his brain.

At the back of the safe were packets of dollar bills.

He took one out. Each bill was for $100.00; there were at least a hundred bills. There were ten packets of the same size. The notes were held together with broad rubber bands, but were not new.

What was Haffmeyer doing with so much money here? Were these his pieces of silver?

The discovery and the question prised Dawlish's mind from alertness, made the moment of greatest danger. The danger came, swooping. He heard the slight sound at the french window, and spun round.

A woman with a gun stood there, the gun pointing.

At first, that was all he saw and knew. Soon, he was to see the woman's beauty, to realize that she was looking at him with a fixed intensity from tawny eyes. Now, all he saw and thought about was the gun. It was large for her hand, but she held it steady.

Dawlish stood up, slowly.

He was huge and massive, with crinkly fair hair and a face which would have been handsome but for a broken nose. His eyes were cornflower blue, somehow the eyes of a child; that was due to their candour.

People who feared him because of his gigantic size were often reassured by those candid eyes.

The woman looked past him; for the first time he saw that she was young—not yet thirty, anyhow. Her dress was green.

'Is he dead?' she asked, as if without fear.

'Yes.'

'Did you kill him?'

'No. I wanted to talk to him.'

'Who *are* you?'

'Never mind,' Dawlish said.

She looked back at him as he began to move towards her. He didn't stop, although the gun still covered him. He showed an apologetic kind of smile.

'Don't come any nearer,' she said; so his size did not worry her.

He stopped.

'They'll say I did it,' said the woman.

'Didn't you?' asked Dawlish, gently.

She glanced at the dead man again.

'I ought to have killed him,' she said. 'I hated him enough. I don't know why I didn't kill him long ago. They all know what I thought about him. They'll say that I did do this.'

Dawlish took a step forward.

'If you didn't, does it matter what they say?'

'Listen,' she said, 'I didn't kill him, but what's to stop me from killing you?' She drew back a pace, out of reach. The gun was very steady, covering his chest. There was no expression on her face—no fear, no lust for blood, nothing but the bright shell of her beauty. Even then, with her finger on the trigger, when a slight tensing of her muscles might send him to find out just where Haffmeyer had gone, Dawlish began to perceive how beautiful she was. It was easy to believe that she had been given every gift that God could give her—except vitality. Her eyes were as dull and her face as blank as that.

'If I kill you,' she said, 'I could say I came here and found you with him.'

'And it would be true,' Dawlish said.

She nodded slowly.

'That's right, it would be true.' A faint spark of interest showed in her eyes. 'So what's stopping me?'

'Some people can kill a man easily as if they were swatting a fly,' Dawlish said, in a gentle, conversational voice, 'and others can't bring themselves to kill the fly. Haffmeyer was in the first category.' He glanced at Haffmeyer. 'I don't think that anyone should die for killing him, do you?'

'No,' she said. But she might shoot, the danger was close pressing.

Dawlish went a step nearer. The gun still covered him, but

was just within his reach. It depended who could move first—the woman by just squeezing the trigger, or he by swinging his arm round to knock the gun to one side.

'Don't crowd me,' she warned, and the gun moved an inch.

Dawlish backed away again, but not very far. It was easy to imagine that Haffmeyer was sitting behind him, gloating, mocking. It was even easier to see the perfection of the woman's skin—which was the colour of pale honey—and the beauty of her tawny eyes. If only life would spark in them, they would be magnificent eyes.

A new sound came into the quiet.

He knew that she heard it, although she did not glance behind her, towards the garden and the forest.

A car was coming along the road.

The beat of its engine grew louder. Soon the glow of its headlights showed, faint at first, and then bright against the branches of trees. It swayed up and down wildly, for the car was travelling at speed.

It passed.

The woman relaxed—as tense as Dawlish, as fearful of the police. It was the first moment when he really had a chance to act, when he could hope to reach the gun before she squeezed. Yet if he swung his arm, her pressure on the trigger would be almost a reflex action.

He stepped towards her casually, and was almost level when he flicked his right hand towards hers, encircling her slim wrist with his powerful fingers. Her hand, her fingers and her body stiffened. A shot roared, a bullet bit into the floor. The smell of cordite was in Dawlish's nostrils as he twisted and the gun fell from her grasp. As it touched the floor he kicked at it; it slid across the room and hit the wall, bounced back an inch, and stopped.

'Sorry,' Dawlish said, and let go her wrist. He moved away, and picked up the gun.

'Who are you?'

She still wasn't really frightened of him.

He noticed her hair, for the first time. Before, he had known that it was attractive hair. Now he discovered that it was a rich auburn, glowing, rippling, drawn back from her forehead, then falling almost to her shoulders.

She didn't speak.

'Who are you?' asked Dawlish. 'And do you mind if we go outside?'

'I'm his wife,' she said, but didn't move.

Involuntarily, Dawlish glanced towards Haffmeyer. No one could ever have called Haffmeyer a good-looking man; there were those who thought him grotesque. What strange force had joined this beauty to that beast?

'I see,' Dawlish said gravely. 'I'm sorry about this, but we have to go.'

'Where?'

'Does it matter? I must get away from here.'

'Don't you think I want to get away?' she asked with sudden vehemence. 'If the police come they'll think I killed him; they wouldn't believe me if I told them about you.'

She spoke as if she knew that the dice were heavily loaded against her, and that she would never have a fair chance. Only the fatalism bred of that belief could have made her speak like that. Dawlish could have told her that there was all the evidence a third-rate policeman would need to say that a second person had been in the room. He didn't.

'I must take some clothes,' she said. 'And—'

She moved suddenly, no more afraid of the gun than she would have been had she been sure that it wasn't loaded. She hurried to a cabinet and poured herself a drink of Scotch. Then she moved again to the safe, and went down on one knee. The grace of her movement was exquisite. Her right leg, thrust backwards beneath the falling three-quarter-length gown, had the kind of beauty which can blind a man to everything else. She moved swiftly, picking up the packets of 100-dollar bills. Cradling them, she stood up and moved towards Dawlish.

'Open the door, quickly.'

He turned and obeyed her, and she hurried out of the study into the large hall. Dawlish was close behind her. She walked swiftly to the stairs, and started up, knowing exactly what she wanted to do.

He followed.

Her footsteps rang, his rapped, on the bare pine boards of the landing; were softened by a bearskin rug, then sounded clear again. She went a few yards along a passage, and kicked a door open. For a moment, she disappeared from his sight. Dawlish went forward swiftly, the gun poised—but he need not have worried. Haffmeyer's wife was standing by the side of a bed, letting the packets fall on to it. Fierce vitality had come into her eyes and her face now.

'Get me that grip,' she said, and pointed towards the wardrobe. She went to the dressing-table, pulled open a drawer and snatched out clothes—flimsy nylon things. She flung these behind her, to the nearer bed.

Dawlish took the valise from the top of the wardrobe.

'Why don't you pack these for me?' she said, and straightened up. There was the urgency of desperation in her movements. She wanted to get away, above all things. She was afraid of what would happen to her when the police discovered that her husband was dead.

More—she was sure that they would start to look for her.

'Hurry, please,' she pleaded.

She crossed to the wardrobe, opened it, bent down and took out two pairs of shoes and a pair of slippers, then took several dresses out, on their hangers.

'Do you have a window arm in your car?' she asked abruptly.

'No.'

'You'll just have to fit ours on.' She glanced at him as he put the flimsies into the valise, and then she crossed to the bathroom. The door was ajar. She didn't close it, just collected what she needed, and came back with her hands laden. Excitement burned in her eyes, and that was more important now than the earlier fear.

'I'll take the dresses,' she said, and hurried towards the door.

What would she have done, Dawlish wondered, if she could read his thoughts? She could describe him to the police. She could tell a convincing story. She would be able to describe not only what he looked like, but how he spoke—with the quiet, English voice which contrasted sharply with her own, with Haffmeyer's, with everyone's out here.

What would she say if she knew that he dared not let her go?

And what would she say if she knew that he wondered how much of what she was doing was due to fear, excitement, eagerness—and how much of that was pretence, because she was as anxious to watch him as he was to watch her?

CHAPTER II

DANGER

Dawlish put out the hall light.

Haffmeyer's wife stepped from the loggia on to the gravel drive, which showed up pale beneath the stars; and then on to the sweeping stretch of grass which led to the road.

The darkness was broken by her flashlight. She shone it downwards. Now and again, her foot appeared in it, then was lost in the blackness beyond the beam. He followed her, closely, his own flashlight in his left hand, his gun in his right, hers in his pocket. She moved towards the garage which was built at the side of the house. Now her feet crunched on the gravel again.

Crickets sang.

Here and there, an owl hooted its mournful defiance to the massed trees.

The woman stopped.

'Where is your car?' He guessed that she was looking over her shoulder.

'Among the trees, on the other side of the road.'

'That so?' she said, and he thought that she was mildly

amused. Since she had begun to move, there was plenty of life in her. She waited for him. 'You open the door, I'll hold the flashlight.'

'I'd rather we did it the other way round.'

'I'm as anxious to get away from here as you are,' she said, as if irritated, 'but no one's on my tail, yet.' She did what he told her, nevertheless, while he shone his flashlight. In the bright light the whiteness of her hands and the scarlet of her nails showed up vividly.

It was warm.

Moths fluttered about the torch beam, wings like beaten gold, eyes showing tiny spots of pink.

The door slid open. Two cars were inside the garage. When she switched on the light, Dawlish saw that one was a blue Buick, the other a red Pontiac. She went between the two cars and opened the back door of the Buick, leaning inside. Her body was half hidden; her face was in light and shade at the same time. She moved one leg, to kneel inside the car. He studied the other.

She backed out, with a metal window-arm in her hand.

As she drew level with him, Dawlish put out the light. He switched on his torch—then switched it off again. They stood quite still.

'Close the door,' Dawlish whispered.

She obeyed; the door seemed much noisier than when she had opened it. Two owls hooted, as if in melancholy conspiracy. The crickets shrilled their message.

The dark sky was pale, not far off, with the headlights of a car which drew nearer, until they could hear the engine. It showed the trees, pine and chestnut, with clumps of spruce here and there, against the faint glow. As that grew brighter and the trees against it darker, Dawlish took the woman's arm.

They moved together, towards the trees near the drive. The house was on a plot which had been cut out of the forest. It was sheltered, secluded, lonely. Soon they could see the whiteness of the light shining through the trees; tree upon tree showed as a black trunk, then vanished, only to be replaced by others; it was as if the trees were running.

The car slowed down.

'They're coming here,' she whispered, and fear was back in her again.

'Who was Haffmeyer expecting?'

'I don't know.'

'Think.'

'He didn't say he was expecting anybody,' she said.

The car was almost level, moving very slowly now. It was swinging, to enter the drive gates. The shining lights made silver of the lawns, the swimming pool, the mesh around the tennis courts. Then they shone upon the white frame walls, reflecting yellow against the wide windows, on the yellow of the door.

Gravel crunched, and the car stopped ten yards from that door.

'Wait here,' Dawlish whispered.

He moved forward, the noise he made drowned by the greater noise that the man from the other car made on the gravel. There appeared to be only one. The headlights were still on, and the man showed up clearly, stocky, vigorous of movement, wearing a pale grey suit and a hat with a wide brim. He sprang up to the loggia, reached the door, and pressed the bell.

Dawlish heard it ring.

There was no way he could get from the lawn to the loggia without stepping on gravel, and now there was no sound to drown whatever he made. He went as near as he could. The man stood with his back towards him.

The man pressed again.

Dawlish took two steps forward. He couldn't be sure whether the man noticed anything, but he saw the right hand go towards the pocket. If he moved further to the right, Dawlish would step into the beam of the headlights, and his shadow would give him away. Gun poised, he ventured another step forward.

The man spun round, his gun raised.

'Stay there!'

Dawlish sensed the man was trigger-jumpy, moved to one side, then fired. His target was clear and compact. The square face was set, the eyes were narrowed against the glare. Dawlish's bullet struck the man's gun arm. The gun dropped. Dawlish leapt and reached the loggia.

'Turn round.'

'The hell—'

Dawlish hit him; a giant hitting an ordinary man. The stranger gave a gasping cry, and turned round. He had courage; fear of Dawlish showed in his eyes, but he kept his voice steady.

'This is one of your mistakes—I'm a police officer, and—'

Dawlish didn't speak. His voice would give him away if he talked too much. He simply struck the man on the jaw; he needed to strike only once, and heard the grunt before the man fell.

His movements gave an impression of great power held on a leash.

'Don't—' began Mrs. Haffmeyer.

She was just behind him, and Dawlish hadn't heard her come. That was bad, because he should have heard every sound. That was twice tonight that he had concentrated on one thing so much that he had been unaware of others.

He reminded himself that the mission was vital to his future; and perhaps only he in the whole wide world could carry it out.

'Don't what?'

'Kill him.'

'You needn't worry about that,' Dawlish said, more calmly than he felt. 'Just watch the road.'

'But—'

'Turn round, and watch it.'

She obeyed.

Dawlish bent over the man, took off his coat, and saw that the wound in the arm had missed the bone and artery. He ripped the man's own shirt to make a bandage; another strip to gag him. Then he began to go through the fallen man's pockets. There were the usual oddments of money, cigarettes, lighter, penknife, handkerchief. Dawlish turned him over, so that his face showed—an odd, grotesque pattern of light and shade in the merciless glow of the headlights. It was a broad, swarthy face; the mouth was long and thin—the upper lip was particularly thin, the lower thrust forward slightly. The chin was massive, the nose short and blunt, the eyebrows jutting and jet black. The close-cropped hair looked black, too.

Dawlish would never forget that face.

Haffmeyer's wife would never forget his, either. She had seen it too often. She would be able to describe it in detail. So she could be dangerous.

'Hurry,' she urged.

Was she frightened because she *had* killed her husband?

'I've nearly finished.' Dawlish had only one more pocket to go through. He found a card in a slit pocket that it would have been easy to overlook. He took the card out, and read it—and began to smile. There was a photograph of the man who lay unconscious, and the card showed that he was from the Federal Bureau of Investigation.

Dawlish slipped it into his own pocket.

'*Hurry,*' the woman breathed.

'Coming.' But he wasn't quite ready. He took coils of cord from his hip pocket, wound one round the man's wrists, the other round his ankles, then bent down and hoisted the man to his shoulders.

Mrs. Haffmeyer caught her breath; as anyone might who saw a giant lift a full-grown man as if he were a bag of feathers.

Dawlish said: 'Go ahead, shining the torch. Switch it out if another car comes.'

She turned and obeyed. It couldn't be easy for her. She had the dresses draped over her shoulder, carried the valise—and the torch at the same time. Its movements were snakelike and unpredictable, but it showed the way. They reached the road.

Twenty yards along, Dawlish said:

'Turn off the road, now.'

She obeyed. In a moment, the beam of light shone on the black of Dawlish's Mercury. Soon they were by the side of the car. Dawlish opened the rear door, lowered his prisoner, and shoved him inside—making no special effort, and using his great strength casually, he propped the man up in a corner, with his head lolling on his chest.

'Give me those.' He turned and held out his arm for the valise, put it in, then took the dresses and put them in the car 'We'll fix the window-arm later,' he said. 'Get in.' He went round to the other side, and got in—both doors slammed together. He switched on the headlights, and the trees showed up like black poles. Then he switched off again, and looked in all directions, seeing no glow of light. He backed out of the little clearing.

'What are you going to do with him?'

'With Kell?'

'Who said his name is Kell?'

'His card,' Dawlish said. His voice was casual and deceptively soft. The women couldn't see it, but there was a curve at his lips, as if he were amused. 'Put him off, when we're the other side of Wolf Creek.'

'Why wait?'

'It's lonelier there,' Dawlish said. 'If anyone finds him, it will take longer for him to telephone the police. How soon would you expect anyone to find your husband?'

'He has a lot of visitors,' she said.

'Servants?'

'There's only Mo' and Lizzie. They'll arrive around eight o'clock tomorrow, maybe a little later.'

'Why don't they sleep in?'

'He doesn't want anyone sleeping in.'

'Do you help to entertain his guests?'

'Some of them,' she admitted. 'Some of them I don't see. I don't want to talk about it.'

'Please yourself,' Dawlish said. 'You'll find cigarettes in the dashboard pocket.'

She sounded startled. 'In the where?'

He grinned. 'In the glove compartment.'

'Oh,' she said.

Nine women in ten, ninety-nine in a hundred, would surely have asked him where he came from. She didn't. She took out the cigarettes and a book of matches, lit a cigarette and handed it to him.

'Thanks.' He put it to his lips.

Smoking, they sat in silence except for the purring of the engine. The beams in front carved a tunnel out of the night, between the trees. Now and again there was a bump against the windscreen as they killed a moth or beetle. Dawlish drove fast but cornered with care. In a few minutes, lights showed ahead of them—all brightly coloured neon. They swung off the dirt road on to bitumen, then passed a gas station, which was lit up brightly. A man lounged against the gas pump, and seemed to be watching them.

He fell behind.

Dawlish turned right, on to Highway 99. Lights and people showed up, traffic lights stopped them. In the back sat the unconscious Kell, head lolling on his chest, easy for anyone to see.

The lights seemed to stay red for a long time, but turned at last.

Dawlish heard the woman's long expulsion of breath as they started off again. She was keyed up as tautly as anyone could be. She was likely to break under any kind of pressure—and to do the wrong thing. He was going to put out Kell, who couldn't have recognized him and therefore wasn't really dangerous. He ought to put the woman off at the same time.

His thoughts were clear, the issues plain—but her motives weren't. Haffmeyer had lied and branded him; Haffmeyer's wife might be able to prove that, and if she were in his debt she was more likely to try to help. Had she hated her husband enough to kill him? Was she a greater menace than a likely help?

Surely she would know something about Haffmeyer? His friends, his employers perhaps, who had paid him to brand Dawlish, in sworn evidence, as a traitor to England *and* as an enemy of the United States.

There was a moment for decision and a moment for action. He decided that this was not the moment for action with Haffmeyer's wife. He drove slowly until they were out of the speed zone, and then sent the car surging forward.

Eight miles out of Wolf Creek, he saw a side road, took it, and was soon lost among the forest and on a winding dirt road.

No one followed them.

CHAPTER III

BREAKFAST

'We'll stop and have some breakfast soon,' Dawlish said.

Haffmeyer's wife didn't answer.

He glanced at her. She was leaning towards the window, her head on one side, moving gently up and down with the swaying of the car. The hair fell back from her cheek and her ear. He looked at her again and again. She was so peaceful now. Everything about her was beautiful, from the way her hand rested against her leg to the way her lashes fell upon her cheek.

It was daylight.

There was more traffic now, some of it passing them, none of the drivers taking any notice of them. Why should they? The road here was straight, but there had been many twists and turns. They couldn't be far from the Pacific Coast. They were a hundred and forty miles from where they had started. It was five hours since they had left Kell—and much of the journey had been as slow as this.

Dawlish slowed down as they neared a corner, turned it, stopped and lit a cigarette.

He smoked as he watched the woman. She was so sound asleep that the ceasing of the movement did not disturb her. He watched the rise and fall of her breasts. He looked at the bloom of her skin. Morning light could be cruel, and they were at a stretch of road which faced east, into the rising sun; but no light could be cruel to her. Yet beneath her eyes there were shadowy patches, and her sleep was the sleep of exhaustion. Now that he let himself think, he recalled that she had behaved as if she were at the end of all endurance. That emptiness, that slowness of speech, the difficulty with which she had made up her mind, told the same story. She had flogged herself to keep awake. The only time she had been at all energetic had been after the drink.

He finished the cigarette.

He knew a little, a very little, about the country. He had friends here, but dare not call upon them for help, for they might think it their duty to betray him. This was his task alone, his risk to take.

He wondered again—could she help? Why had she behaved so?

A car passed, the driver glancing curiously at him. He lit another cigarette. He looked at himself in the driving mirror, and was not pleased with what he saw. Tired eyes with bags beneath them; drawn lips; thick yellow stubble; all the indications that unless he slept soon he would exhaust himself.

Dare he sleep, and risk her running away?

Had she really run because she believed the police would think that she had killed her husband? Or because she *had* done so?

He was hungry as well as tired.

He started off again. Not a mile away he came to the outskirts of a small town—two or three gas stations, a restaurant, a dozen shops and twice as many frame-houses. It was early, but they already looked hot. The streets were dusty, and tall trees grew, promising plenty of shade later in the day.

Dawlish drew off the road and parked in front of a restaurant where a neon sign was in futile competition with the sun, declaring in pale red:

OPEN DAY AND NITE STEAKS AS YOU LIKE 'EM

Two or three men were inside. The woman stirred.

'We're going to eat,' Dawlish said. 'Cover that hair, tie a scarf round it. Understand?'

Sleepily, she nodded.

Dawlish went into the restaurant, closing his eyes and opening them again, to try to ease the ache. There was a counter with stools in front of it, and tables for service—and the clattering sound of a juke box. A man at the counter sat with one elbow resting, and chin in his hand. The man behind the counter beamed at Dawlish and said:

'Morning, sir!'

'Hallo,' Dawlish said.

It was just one word, and the music should have drowned his accent. But the man with his chin in his hand turned to look, and the brisk man behind the counter came hurrying, beaming. He was dressed in white clothes which looked as if they had come straight from the laundry that morning.

'What'll you have?' he inquired brightly. 'Bacon and eggs and'—he paused to grin—'*tea*?'

He was one of the clever, the discerning ones, Dawlish thought grimly. This was part of the trouble—his voice. He could speak five languages fluently and get along in several others, but no one in this world would ever mistake him for an American. It was one of the things that couldn't be avoided. An American would have been as noticeable in England, where part of the job had already been done.

He would have to brazen this out.

'If you can make tea!'

'Sure can, sir, with red-hot water.'

Dawlish found himself smiling.

'That sounds fine.'

The tune came to an end. The record dropped into place. The big clean restaurant was oddly, utterly silent. The man with his chin in his hand looked at Dawlish; so did the man who had put the money in the juke box.

Then all of them looked towards the door.

It opened, and Haffmeyer's wife came in.

She had a scarf tied round her hair, and her eyebrows looked darker than before. She could not hide the fact that she had just woken up, and stifled a yawn. There was a mistiness about her eyes which made her seem very young and innocent, and she was probably much more young than innocent. She walked as if all the grace of women had been given to her.

Each man here watched her. She appeared to be oblivious of all except Dawlish. She came towards him and slid into a chair next to him, and gave a slow, sensuous smile. She put her hand on his.

'After sleep, I need to eat,' she said.

'That order for two?' asked the bright counter-hand.

'Bacon and eggs?' Dawlish asked her.

'Sure, honey,' she said. She leaned against him—not too heavily, but enough to make everyone else in the restaurant know what she was doing. She wasn't really oblivious of them, she enjoyed the thrill which their interest gave her. She expected this silent adoration, and certainly she received it.

Dawlish gave her a cigarette.

'Thanks,' she said, and accepted a light.

The man at the counter turned away and dropped his chin

on his hand again. It was a long, pointed chin. No one now appeared to be looking at them. But not one of the three would forget her. Probably each would carry a picture of her to his dying day, one that would get hazier, fading as a dream—a dream of perfection. Hers was that kind of face. They would remember him, too, because of his voice and because he had been with her. When the police began their inquiries, they would talk. He wondered how long it would be before police were stopping all black Mercury cars to look at the driver and passenger.

The counter-hand came again with water, knives and forks, and a paper serviette with a map on it, and the legend:

THE REDWOOD HIGHWAY *to the* REDWOOD EMPIRE

She was still very close to him.

'Don't misunderstand me,' she said, 'but it's time I knew your first name, I may have to use it sometimes.'

Glancing down, he saw the gleam of laughter in the tawny eyes. She was amused. It would probably always amuse her to have a man at the end of a piece of string. But there was something he liked about her, and it wasn't just her beauty. He had the feeling that had their lives crossed somewhere else at some other time, they would have been good friends.

'Pat for Patrick,' he said.

'Pat what?'

'Smith.'

Her eyes laughed again. They were much clearer now that she had slept.

'All right, Pat for Patrick Smith, have it your own way. I'm known as—'

She didn't finish, because Dawlish jerked her elbow. Bacon

and eggs, sizzling on the plate, appeared in front of them, with delicate-looking white toast. There was coffee; and tea, with a tea-bag at the bottom of a big cup. The water looked almost boiling, the tea was infusing well.

'You'll sure enjoy that if you're hungry,' the counter-hand said. He didn't move away immediately, although there was no need for him to stay; it was the beauty of the woman which held him. Then he hurried off, as if he knew that he wouldn't get free from her unless he made a spirited effort.

Behind the counter, he twiddled with the dial of a radio. A girl was singing, *If I can't have it my way, then I'll try it your way,* and then there was a crackle and a man's voice.

'. . . That's all you have to do, folk, just go into your favourite drugstore and ask for it. Now don't forget the name—Peppo. Supposing we say that all together, huh? One, two, three—'

A chorus joined in with a roar: 'PEPPO!'

'Man and woman, boy and girl, Peppo's the drink you'll like more than any other drink in the world, folk. Don't forget—'

'PEPPO!' came the chorus.

Dawlish's plate was nearly empty; so was the woman's.

'And here's a news flash, folk, coming to you with the courtesy of Peppo—the drink you'll like more than any other drink in the world. Early this morning famous scientist Professor Gurth Haffmeyer, of Lone Wolf, Wolf County, Washington, was found murdered in his study—dead in the room where many of his breath-taking discoveries have been made. The Professor was shot in the head. Professor Haffmeyer married beautiful model Vanessa del Mio eight months ago and they lived . . . The Wolf County Police would like Mrs. Haffmeyer to call them from wherever she is, right now, and in case she doesn't receive this message, this is what she looks like— stand by, folk, for a description of Mrs. Haffmeyer, wife of the murdered scientist, by the courtesy of Peppo. Height, five seven, weight around a hundred and forty, auburn hair, amber-coloured eyes. . . .'

'Don't get up,' Dawlish said.

He picked up her coffee cup and his tea, and sauntered towards the counter. The counter-hand was looking at Vanessa Haffmeyer. The man with his chin on his hand was looking at Vanessa. Thank God her hair was covered with the scarf.

The other man got up and went slowly towards the door. From the window, he looked at Vanessa.

'More coffee, please,' Dawlish said by the counter, 'and this time I'll have coffee, too.'

'Y-y-yessir!'

'And I'll have a packet of Camels,' Dawlish added, and stifled a yawn. 'Is there a hotel near here?'

'There ain't no hotels, there's plenty of motels, I guess—any one of them's good.' The counter-hand was pouring the coffee. 'You only have to go a little way and you'll come to Astoria; you'll find all you want there, I guess.'

'Thanks,' said Dawlish.

He went back to the seat. The man who had left was standing outside, looking at the Mercury. Two other men walked past, with slow, easy gait. Two cars and a big dog passed. The man walked out of sight, while Dawlish sipped his coffee but didn't sit down again.

'You come after me,' he said. 'In a few minutes.'

'Sure, Pat.' Her voice was surprisingly calm. She must know that everyone who had seen her wondered if she were Vanessa Haffmeyer.

The check was two dollars seventy cents. Dawlish put three-fifty down, and went out. Vanessa reached a corner and a door which said *Powder Room*. Dawlish stepped into the open. It was much warmer, and would soon be hot. There wasn't a cloud in the sky.

The man who left the restaurant was out of sight, but there weren't many places where he could go.

He was in a drugstore nearly next door; there would be a telephone in there.

The man was in a telephone booth, looking towards Dawlish—as if he were frightened out of his wits. Dawlish nodded to him, bought another pack of Camels and then sauntered out. He took the car to the nearest gas station, only fifty yards down the main street; it was being filled when Vanessa appeared. She didn't hurry, either.

He paid the boy, who hurried to clean his windscreen; then started the engine.

'We're on the run,' he said to Vanessa.

'Don't I know it!'

'The man telephoned someone, probably the police. I imagine the nearest police are at Astoria—a few miles on. We'll drive that way to start with, then double back on a side road. As soon as we can, we'll get another car or take a bus—we can't go much further in the Mercury.' Dawlish had his foot hard on the accelerator now, and they were travelling very fast. He swung off the main road at the first chance, drove for miles at high speed, and struck another wide highway.

It wasn't long before they came within sight of the city limits of a town.

On either side of the road were motor-courts. Cars were drawn up outside the chalets which had been let for the night. He pulled into the largest, on the outskirts of the small town, drove straight up to a front door outside which there was no car and said:

'Do they let you use these places by day?'

'Any time,' said Vanessa.

'Good. Stay here.' He got out, and strolled towards the end chalet, where a sign said *Office*. An old man without any hair, wearing a T-shirt and faded jeans, came out of the front door, smiling a greeting.

'You been driving through the night?'

'Yes, pretty fast,' Dawlish said.

'That so,' said the old man, and was obviously intrigued by the accent. 'Well, our beds are mighty comfortable; you'll catch up on sleep. You like one bed or two?'

'Two,' Dawlish said.

'Then you'll have to move your car, mister, the one right there has a big bed.' He pointed. 'Chalet with a double bed is one-fifty cheaper.'

'I'll move the car, thanks,' Dawlish said.

He heard the first wail of a siren, not far off. The old man didn't even turn his head, but went inside, picked a key off a board, which had dozens on it, and came out again. The siren was going up and down wildly. Dawlish made himself turn with the old man. A car swept past, and its siren began to fade. Another car with uniformed men in it also passed. Dawlish saw that out of the corner of his eye, as they stopped in front of a chalet.

It had a large room with two beds, a shower and hand-basin, was pleasantly furnished, and had a faint smell of pines.

'. . . and air-conditioning,' the old man said proudly. 'We don't need it much by night, but sometimes by day it gets mighty hot up here.'

'I expect it does,' said Dawlish.

He could still hear the siren in the distance.

'Come and pay me when you've settled in,' said the old man, and moved off towards the office.

Dawlish got into the car. Vanessa was smoking a cigarette. She sat very still, and Dawlish imagined that the echo of the siren was still in her ears, too. He drove to the chalet on the other side and pulled up so that she could get out and step into the room without being seen except by anyone who happened to come out of a nearby chalet.

'Just take your clothes,' he said, 'I'll bring the rest.'

She nodded.

He did not have to tell her to carry the dresses so that they hid her face. He went to the back of the car and took out her valise; and then opened the back, for his own case. He carried them both into the chalet room. She was hanging the dresses, which were on hangers, behind a plastic curtain which served as a wardrobe.

Dawlish shut the door with his foot.

'If they search this town, how long do you think it will be before they find us?' Vanessa asked.

Her mood was very different from what it had been; she was badly frightened. She dropped on to the end of a bed.

'Keep your hair covered and darken your eyebrows,' Dawlish said. 'You can't do much with a face like that. We'll dye your hair when we can.' He lit a cigarette. He was smoking too much, but that didn't surprise him and this wasn't the time to worry about it. 'Nothing can stop you from being beautiful, and from now on they'll know we're together.' He drew very hard at the cigarette.

At least four people could describe him now; they were probably doing that to the police already.

'Pat,' she said, 'we haven't a chance, and you know we haven't.'

'If your hair were a different colour and we had a different car, we would have a chance,' said Dawlish easily. 'It's important to me that we don't get caught.' He smiled faintly. 'Didn't I make that clear before?'

'Important to *you*,' she said in a funny voice. 'What do you think—?'

She didn't finish, but got up and began to walk round the room, as if the thought of keeping still terrified her.

'I didn't kill him,' she asserted challengingly. 'I hated everything about him. I would have killed him if I could have found the courage; I just couldn't get as far as that. He was everything that's bad. But I don't want to die for him.' She stopped suddenly, close to him, and faced him with her eyes blazing. 'And I don't want you to die for him, even if you killed him. But we haven't got a chance.'

'We have to make our chance,' Dawlish said. 'And we have to get another car.'

'They grow on trees,' she said bitterly. 'I—'

She stopped.

A siren howled in the distance, grew louder, grew so loud that Dawlish himself would have found it easy to scream; and then faded. As its last banshee note ended there was a sharp knock at the door.

Vanessa started violently, moved to Dawlish and gripped his arm.

The knock came again.

CHAPTER IV

THE STRANGER

Dawlish prised himself free from Vanessa's grip. He moved towards the door. She turned suddenly, and he guessed that she was looking for a gun in his case, but there wasn't one there. He reached the door. Against the window he could see the shadow of a man.

He opened the door several inches, standing to one side; he had known the time he had opened a door and had a bullet snarl at him.

A man stood there, hat on the back of his head, thumbs hooked over his belt. He wore a loose-fitting shirt, no coat, narrow purple jeans. He wasn't Kell of the F.B.I. but he had that kind of look, and there was a glint in his pale grey eyes. He was chewing. He didn't smile, but raised his head a little to look into Dawlish's eyes.

'Hi, Patrick,' he greeted.

Dawlish didn't speak or close the door. The man put a foot forward, to make sure that the door couldn't close.

'We can talk,' he said, 'or I can telephone the police and tell them you're here. How would you like that?' He kept chewing. 'How would Vanessa like it?'

Dawlish opened the door, keeping his right hand at his pocket about his gun. The man came in, closed the door and leaned against it, with his thumbs still hooked in his belt.

'Hi, Vanessa,' he said, and looked her up and down insolently. His gaze lingered on her face. When he smiled, it was with a kind of reluctant admiration.

'So you can have everything,' he said. 'But I'm ashamed of you, Patrick. And you a married man.'

Dawlish just stood watching, wary.

'Did he tell you he was married, Vanessa?' asked the stranger. 'Before he persuaded you to shoot Gurth and then run away with him?'

She said thinly, 'That's not true, that's a lie.'

'Think so? Think anyone would believe it?' The man shook his head slowly. 'No one in this world and certainly no one in the State of Washington would believe it, Vanessa. The two of you worked together and killed the poor unwanted husband, then made off together. So we can have the two of you put away, and we would have plenty to rejoice at.' Still chewing rhythmically, he gave a slow, reluctant smile.

He hadn't a bad face—fresh-coloured, with a heavy jaw and a blunt nose, like Kell, but with better lips and eyes which could smile, although they could also hold a mean look. His hat showed a dark ridge on his forehead, and hair that was nearly ginger.

'With the police you haven't a chance,' he said. 'With me, you've one of a kind. It isn't much of a one, but it's all you've got.'

'Tell me about the chance,' Dawlish said mildly.

'My jeloppy's outside, across the road,' the man told him, 'and Vanessa can go and get in it. There's a driver. He'll take her where she has to go. You can drive me in your car, Patrick, and

I'll tell *you* where to go. You were reported as being together at the restaurant—you'll be safer if you're parted.'

'There's something in that,' Dawlish agreed.

'Pat—' Vanessa began, and caught her breath.

'Pat,' echoed the man with the heavy chin. 'That sounds fine. Pat, short for Patrick. Would you like to know his whole name, Vanessa? He's Patrick Dawlish, because his grandpapa on one side was Irish, but he's as English as they come. That makes him dumb *and* crazy.' He took one thumb from his belt and tapped his forehead. 'He thought he could come here and get away with this!'

Dawlish didn't speak.

The girl looked at him.

The other man said: 'There just isn't any other chance for you—only my way. Stay here, and I'll send for the police. They can be here in three or four minutes. Just please yourself.'

He moved forward, opened the door, winked at Vanessa and then went out.

The door swung to.

Dawlish glanced down at the bulge in his pocket, then slowly released the gun and took his hand out. Vanessa didn't move. Her valise was open, all the things that Dawlish had packed were showing. Her dresses were hanging behind the plastic curtain. Dawlish's case hadn't been touched and still stood at the foot of the bed.

'So we—have to obey him?' Vanessa asked.

She knew that there was really no point in the question; there was nothing else to do. In her fear, her eyes were enormous.

'Do you know him?' Dawlish asked.

'He came to see—Gurth.'

'Often?'

'Two or three times.'

'What's his name?'

'I heard Gurth call him Victor,' Vanessa said. 'Sometimes it was just Vic. Don't ask me what they talked about, I don't know. Whenever we had a guest he didn't want me to see much of, I was locked in my room. Once—'

There was a tap at the door.

'Didn't I tell you to hurry?' came Victor's voice. 'You couldn't have heard me.'

The little old man stood in his T-shirt and jeans, watching, puzzled, as Vanessa walked towards the car on the other side of the road. Dawlish didn't know the make, only that it was brilliant red. Vanessa carried the valise, but not her dresses; Dawlish had those over one arm, his case in the other. Victor stood by, chewing.

'I've had some bad news,' Dawlish said to the old man. 'We can't stay.' He put the case down and handed over a five-dollar bill.

'I'm sorry about that,' the man said, and puzzled or not he became much more cheerful. 'I'm real sorry its bad news, mister.'

'We all are,' Victor said. He picked up the case and put it in the back of the car. Dawlish took the wheel. Victor slid into the seat beside him. 'Don't drive too fast, Patrick.'

Dawlish started the engine and let in the clutch. He saw the red car moving away from the town, and turned after it. The road was winding and pleasant, and the trees grew close to the side. Now and again they caught a glimpse of the Pacific, on the right, a blue haze with diamonds in it. The scarlet car was out of sight; that didn't seem to worry Victor.

'A mile along you come to a fork,' he said. 'Take the right fork.'

'That's towards the sea.'

'They told me how clever you were,' Victor said. 'I don't need reminding.'

Dawlish said, 'I'm not so clever,' and gave a little apologetic smile, then stamped on the brake.

He was ready for the violent jolt; Victor should have been ready for anything, but wasn't. His forehead smacked against the windscreen as Dawlish's bumped lightly. The engine stalled. Dawlish swung off the road and on to the grass, turned and snatched a gun from Victor's limp fingers. The man was dazed but not unconscious.

'What I ought to do is break your neck,' Dawlish said mildly. He shifted his position, and clipped the man beneath the jaw. He heard the teeth snap together. Victor slumped down; he was likely to be unconscious for some time. Dawlish started the engine again, pulled back on to the road, and drove as far as the fork.

He turned right, towards the sea.

After five minutes of driving past trees growing close to the sides of the road, with the stillness among the branches disturbed only by flitting birds—here and there one with brilliant plumage—he came within sight of the sea. It was a long way below. To the right and left, trees grew on the edge of cliffs; there was no cliff road. The tall pines were massed in thick array and clothed with the majesty of grandeur. From here, the blue of the sea was deep, intense; and the diamonds scintillated on it as they danced. The water lapped gently against pale yellow sand and the boulders below.

The road sloped downwards sharply.

Dawlish took the corners cautiously, and was ready to stop at a second's notice.

He went round and round, and each corner was a little lower than the next. They were dropping down into some cove or inlet. Who else would be there? If only the driver of the scarlet car and Vanessa, he could cope; if there were others, and this was a camp . . .

He turned another corner.

Beyond, the road was very steep and ran between towering sandstone cliffs. No trees or bushes grew, but there were tufts of long grass. The cove was visible now—and only one car.

Vanessa stood beside it; so did a man who looked short and very broad, and wore a blue cap with a big peak. They were looking upwards.

The red car was pulled to one side, beneath the cliff. The sand looked hard, there, but it was loose nearer the sea; any car which went too far would sink axle deep, unable to move.

At another bend, the cove was cut off for a moment; it soon reappeared. The short, square man was lighting a cigar. Dawlish was near enough now to see the gun in his left hand, the flash of the match as he struck it with his thumb, and the first plume, next a tiny cloud of smoke which seemed just a wisp of grey.

The road, narrow and bumpy, was very steep.

Dawlish put his foot down on the accelerator. The engine roared and the car leapt forward. He saw Vanessa's surge of terror as she tried to get out of the way, but floundered in the sand. The squat man leapt in the other direction. Dawlish flashed past them, one on either side, slowed down, and felt the wheels slithering in the sand.

He flung the door open.

The driver of the red car had fallen, and was twisting round, cigar gone, mouth open and teeth showing, gun pointing. He fired first. The bullet struck the door with a loud clang; another drilled a hole through the toughened glass. Dawlish fired. The angle was difficult, and he missed. The man got to his knees, taking better aim.

A stone curved an arc in the air, close to him. He didn't see it, but Dawlish did. Another followed. Vanessa's aim wasn't bad. The first dropped just in front of the squat man, the other actually touched him on the shoulder. It made him flinch, and gave Dawlish his chance. He fired again.

The driver's gun went spinning from his hand.

'I shouldn't pick it up,' Dawlish said to him. He slid out of the car. 'Thanks, Vanessa.' He smiled at her as she came round the car, looking at the man who had been her target. He had a swarthy slab of a face, and dark bristle covered his cheeks and chin as quills stand out from a porcupine. He had little dark eyes, and a chest so huge that he looked misshapen.

'Get his gun, will you?' Dawlish asked.

Vanessa walked through the loose sand to get it. Walking was difficult, but she picked it up.

'You go to the car,' Dawlish ordered the prisoner.

The glitter in the little dark eyes was the man's only protest. He trudged along obediently. The sun burned down and the sea lapped gently, seductively, against the beach, while above their heads the tall trees stood guard. The cove was small; nothing suggested that many people came here, although against the cliff at one point were the ashes of a fire, a few empty cans, an empty cigarette pack.

'Sit down there,' Dawlish ordered the squat man.

He obeyed slowly, his eyes still sparkling vengefully. With the car door open, Victor sat immediately above the second prisoner, head still on his chest, eyes still closed.

'Now if you watch them from here, Vanessa,' Dawlish said, 'you can shoot either of them if they start getting fresh, Or difficult.'

She didn't speak, but looked at him. Her lips were parted and there was a gleam in her eyes, very different from that in the man's. They looked golden, with the sun on them; and the sun gave a thousand lights to her auburn hair.

Dawlish went to the back of the red car and lifted the boot lid. Inside were two grips, tools, a can of gasoline and odds and ends of rope. He took several of the pieces of rope and closed the boot, then went back to Vanessa. The men hadn't moved.

'Stand up and turn round,' Dawlish ordered the squat man.

He said harshly, 'When I get you—'

'Just tell yourself about it,' Dawlish said, 'Vanessa doesn't want to hear. I said turn round.' His voice was silky, yet one which it wouldn't do to disobey. The man turned. 'Put your arms behind your back,' said Dawlish.

He tied the man's wrists together and secured him to a door-handle; then dragged Victor out, and treated him the same way. He left plenty of slack so that the men could move. During the tying, Victor came round, but when it was done he was still only half conscious. Dawlish backed away, putting his gun into his pocket, and taking out a pack of Camels. He shook one out for Vanessa.

They smoked.

'If the police come down here, they'll get us,' Dawlish observed lightly. 'Short of swimming, there isn't anything else we can do. But they won't search every bay and inlet. If you stay near here, you can watch the approach and our boy-friends for an hour, can't you?'

'What are you planning to do?' she asked. Her lips were still parted. There was something breathless in her manner, and in the way she looked at him; as if she had never seen anything like him in her life before. Perhaps she was contrasting him with the fat hulk of her husband. In spite of his size, he looked lean; was virile as well as massive. There were women who liked that broken nose; more who liked his smile. Now, his blue eyes were bleary.

'Sleep,' he said. 'I'm almost out on my feet.'

'What do you do when you're awake?' she asked.

He grinned.

'I'll find a shady spot,' he told her. 'You keep in the shade, too, don't sit in a spot where the sun will get at you as it moves round.'

He strolled away.

He had to sleep; and it was quiet here and as safe as anywhere. The risk was in trusting Vanessa; he took it, half fearful.

Vanessa watched as he looked for a hollow in the sand, between the great tufts of grass, then went down on his knees and curled up, as a dog might, to rest. His great body relaxed completely. It was warm, but not hot, in the shade. A gentle breeze blew off the sea, and the sea whispered to him. Whenever he opened his eyes, he could see the two cars, the two men and Vanessa. She was sitting against the cliff, skirt spread out, looking comfortable, looking beautiful, smoking.

He kept awake for ten minutes; she didn't stir. How much did she mean? What was in her mind? Soon the two men would start talking; or Victor would. He would talk smoothly, seductively, offering Vanessa much if only she would betray Dawlish. It would be easy enough for her to cut the man free.

Dawlish closed his eyes and let his thoughts drift. There were times when danger and fear meant nothing, when the only thing a man desired was sleep; and he had reached that stage. This was his third day without real rest; with cat-naps helping him to keep going. He'd soon find out if he could trust Vanessa, wouldn't he? His gun was at hand, and he would wake on the instant—fear of death would see to that.

He went to sleep.

The tall trees stood guard above them, the sea washed the fine sand, the sun gave vivid light or caused black shadows. It shone on Victor and the squat man. They had no rest from it, and would get none for hours—if they were allowed to stay there so long. The squat man began to lick his lips. Victor did the same. His eyes were wide open, he was fully conscious now.

Vanessa stopped looking at them, but shifted her position, lying on her stomach and looking out to sea—but seeing Dawlish at the same time. It would have been difficult to be sure whether she was looking at Dawlish or the shimmering blue ocean.

'Vanessa,' Victor called. His voice was very low and dry.

She stared towards the horizon.

'Vanessa, I want a drink.'

She must have heard, but didn't glance towards him.

'Vanessa—'

He began to talk. His voice was soft, insinuating, tempting. She could have money, she could have freedom, she could have safety. He would tell the police that Dawlish had killed Haffmeyer, they could find witnesses, they would prove that she hadn't been at the house when Haffmeyer had been murdered. There was nothing she need worry about and nothing she couldn't have.

His voice grew hoarse and his mouth dry.

'Vanessa—beautiful—. All the money you want, Vanessa—. You needn't be frightened—we'll tell the police—'

His voice died away.

'How about a drink?' the squat man said in a voice that was cracked and hopeless. 'How about a li'l drink, Vanessa?'

She turned to look at them.

'He's the boss,' she said, and pointed to Dawlish. 'Ask him, when he wakes up.'

She shifted her position again, and lit a cigarette. The sun was turning the faces of the men to red—Victor's a turkey red, the other man's a dusky shade. Sweat glistened on their foreheads, cheeks and lips, even through the long stubble of the squat man. It rolled down their faces and their necks, crumpled the collars of their shirts. They couldn't get any shade at all. Their eyes went bleary and then tiny streaks of blood showed in the whites. They leaned against the burning side of the car, and then slumped downwards until the cords chafed at their wrists. They straightened up but didn't keep upright for long.

'Vanessa—Gimme a drink—You don't have to worry.—All the money you want—Vanessa—Drink—*Gimme a drink.*'

Vanessa looked at the squat man.

'Keep quiet,' she said clearly. 'You'll wake him up.'

'*Gimme a drink!*' he screeched at her.

She stood up slowly, with that wonderful grace, and approached him. Standing close, she said:

'I told you to keep quite.'

She slapped him across the face sharply, knocking his head to and fro. He caught his breath and nearly choked.

Then Victor shot out his arms, and the cord dropped from them. Vanessa started back, a scream born and quickly choked as his hands went round her throat.

CHAPTER V

THE BEACH

Victor's hands tightened. Their faces were a foot apart. His fingers dug into her flesh, and she could not breathe. Only a yard away, the squat man stared with his bloodshot eyes popping out of his head.

Then there was a flurry of movement behind them.

Victor looked round, fear leaping into his eyes. Dawlish was coming with long strides, not floundering in the sand. He had a gun in his hand.

'Stop there!' Victor screeched. 'Stop there, or I'll break her neck! I can do it—I'll break her neck!'

She was already unconscious, and her head was drooping backwards, her hair falling like a wavy shield of bronze where the sun put magic lights into it. Victor held her close. Perhaps he thought that she would stop a bullet, that Dawish dared not shoot for fear of shooting her.

Dawlish stood quite still.

Victor's fingers showed like claws round Vanessa's slender throat, and Dawlish knew that the man could squeeze the life out of her; or twist, and break her neck. It could be done.

He found his lips tight; ugly.

'Let her go,' he said. 'If you kill her, I'll make you suffer an hour for every minute you've made her. Just let her go.'

Victor's eyes stormed at him, the bloodshot streaks much bigger now, making him look as if he were touched with insanity. Dawlish's were clear blue, and rested; two hours' sleep was not enough, but it could keep him going for a long time.

'Let her go,' he repeated.

Victor released Vanessa slowly, reluctantly. She drooped downwards, and fell on the sand at his feet.

'Bend down,' Dawlish said, 'and pull her into the shade, Vic. Don't hurt her. Take her by the shoulders.'

Victor did just that, and pulled Vanessa into the shade. The marks of his fingers were still on her throat, but now Dawlish could see the rise and fall of her breasts and a movement at her lips. She would come round soon. He picked up the rope and saw that the ends were frayed; it was old, and by moving it to and fro along the handle Victor had broken it. Dawlish moved back and leaned against the cliff.

'Do you have anything to drink with you?'

'There's beer on ice.' Victor's voice rose as if he couldn't believe his ears.

'Get some,' Dawlish said. 'Give your friend a drink, too. Don't forget that I would gladly slit your throat and listen to you squealing.' He smiled, with that gentle expression which was so utterly deceptive. 'Don't be long—and bring me a bottle.'

Victor hurried as fast as the shifting sand would let him. The squat man looked at him pathetically. He went to the back of the scarlet car, opened the boot, and then opened a box inside. Dawlish shifted his position, so that he could see everything. The box was filled with cans of beer lying on watery ice. Victor took out four cans, and put his hand to his pocket.

Dawlish didn't speak, just kept him covered.

Victor took out a knife, opened a blade, and punched two holes in each can. Then he took four paper cups from the box, and brought cups and beer towards the shade. He set them both on a flat rock.

'Give your friend one first,' Dawlish said. 'Be polite, Victor.'

Victor licked his lips, staring at the beer as if he hadn't had a drink for weeks. But he did what he was told. He had to hold the paper cup in front of the squat man's lips. His hand was unsteady and some of the beer trickled down the chin. Then he turned and hurried back to the rock.

'Help yourself,' Dawlish said. 'One can, Vic.'

Victor snatched it up.

Vanessa stirred, and her eyes fluttered.

'Prop Vanessa up against the cliff,' Dawlish said.

Soon she was sitting there, looking up at Dawlish and fingering her neck. It must be painful, Dawlish knew; it was already red and swollen. She took the beer from Victor, and swallowed slowly and cautiously; she didn't finish the first cup.

'Put it down,' said Dawlish. 'Go back to the car, Vic.'

'No, don't—'

'You'll get hurt,' Dawlish murmured.

Victor moved back over the sand, very slowly. He seemed to flinch when the full force of the sun struck him again. He didn't turn his back on Dawlish. He came up against the car, winced when his hand touched the burning metal, and stood a few inches in front of it.

Dawlish lit a cigarette, bent down and put it between Vanessa's lips.

'It's all right,' he said. 'You'll feel able to swallow again much sooner than you think. Sorry I slept for so long.' He raised his voice. 'Can you hear me, Vic?'

'Yes.'

'It's hot out there,' Dawlish said, in the same slow and gentle voice—the voice which no one could ever mistake for American. 'It will get hotter. From the look of your friend, it won't be long before he gets sun-stroke, he might even go mad.' His smile could not have been more friendly. 'Take your choice between the sun and the shade.'

'What—what do you want?'

'Your story,' Dawlish said. 'All of it. How you came to know I was here. How you found me. What you and Haffmeyer were doing. Where I'll find the rest of your friends.'

The lazy smile was on his lips all the time. It might have deceived some people. It didn't deceive Victor. He looked at the eyes, not the lips. They were cold, and told their own story—of a man who could be, would be, merciless. Perhaps Victor guessed or knew something of the burden on Dawlish's mind.

'You can please yourself,' Dawlish said. 'Sun or shade.'

'I'll tell you all I know,' Victor surrendered.

The prisoners were in the shade now, tied again to the handles of the car which Dawlish had driven. The squat man's eyes were closed, he looked as if he were asleep—as if the sun had drawn all the life out of him. Victor, with one arm free, squatted on a rock with a can of beer and cigarettes in front of him.

The sun was almost directly above the cove. Ten feet from where they sat it turned the sand into a white furnace and even the sea seemed to lap against the furnace and shudder and sizzle as it rolled back. From the trees on the great cliffs above them stillness came.

'That's everything,' Victor said. 'That's everything I can tell you.'

'You've forgotten a little item,' Dawlish said softly.

'I haven't forgotten a thing.'

'How did you know that I was going to see Haffmeyer? How did you know who I was?' Dawlish was still mild.

'Orde told me!'

'Everything?'

'Your name, where you came from, why you were going to work on Haffmeyer. I don't know another thing, Dawlish.'

Dawlish looked at Vanessa.

'Do you believe him?'

'Turn the heat on him again,' she said.

Victor caught his breath, looked at her as if he would never know anything but hatred for her. The other man opened his eyes, and fear lived in them; how they hated the burning, blinding sun!

'I think I believe them,' Dawlish said. 'Orde's at this lumber mill among the redwoods, and Orde seems to be the man I want next. He employed your husband as well, Victor says. Do you know the name?'

'No,' Vanessa said.

'Pity,' Dawlish murmured. 'I'll have to see Orde. But I don't want him warned. Or do I?'

'I won't talk to Orde—' Victor began eagerly.

'You know,' Dawlish said, standing up and turning towards the sea, 'you're a problem, Vic. If I let you go, *you* might be too frightened to tell Orde what happened, but you probably wouldn't. And you might tell the police what car we've borrowed. Yes, you're a problem.'

'They're no problem,' said Vanessa thinly.

Victor gave her that look again—the one of searing hatred, because she seemed a greater menace than Dawlish.

'No?' Dawlish murmured. 'What would you do?'

'Shoot them. Push them over the cliff. Drown them.' She

spoke calmly, but without smiling. She wasn't looking at them, only at Dawlish's profile.

'If you leave them alive,' she said, 'they'll find a way of snarling you.'

'You're probably right.' Dawlish moved away from them towards the sea's edge. She joined him. The gentle breeze blew off the shimmering waves, and pressed her dress against her exciting body. Behind them, the two men watched fearfully. Against the horizon a ship showed in pale silhouette, with smoke rising gently from its one stack and making a tiny smudge against the bold blue of the sky.

The waves, so gentle, still whispered.

'I think I want Orde to know I'm getting closer to him,' Dawlish said at last.

'You can't mean that!'

'I do.' He looked down at her. 'They'll tell Orde. They'll lie about the way they escaped, but they won't about having told me about the lumber mill. Orde will get ready for a visit. He'll feel sure that I can't go to the police. He'll expect me—and be ready for me; and if he's the man I'm after—'

'You ought to catch him by surprise!'

'No,' said Dawlish. 'I can't win that way. I think Orde had better know.'

'You could kill them,' she said, 'and tell Orde about it yourself.'

'Why do you hate them so much, Vanessa?'

'I just want to live. I think I've a better chance if they're dead.'

'Listen,' he said, 'killing isn't a way to save your neck. You're too excited. Calm down.'

'They'll put the police on to us!'

'I don't think so,' Dawlish said.

'Why shouldn't they? This Orde doesn't owe you anything, does he?'

Her face, her body, even the huskiness of her voice, had a beauty which was great enough to hurt, yet she could talk like this and mean it. Dawlish let his thoughts roam over what had happened from the time he had reached Haffmeyer's house, and all that had followed. He remembered the way in which she had surprised and startled him—and avoided giving him the slightest warning that she was near.

Was she as clever as she was beautiful?

'I know what I'll do,' Dawlish said. 'I'll tell Orde where they are. He can send for them.' He found himself smiling, but she didn't smile, she sharply disapproved. 'I'll telephone Orde,' he added slowly, 'or you can. We'll leave Victor and his friend here, in one of the cars, and Orde can send for them if he wants them. If he doesn't—'

'They'll be found on Saturday or Sunday, when the next party comes here to swim and have a barbecue.'

'That's three days. Orde will have sent for them by then,' said Dawlish.

Vanessa didn't speak.

'I'm getting hungry,' Dawlish said, and turned round towards the two men.

They were standing and watching. At the distance of fifty yards, their tension showed clearly—fear was in their eyes. They knew that they might have been sentenced to death, and there was no courage in them. Victor held himself more erect, more boldly. The other man looked as if he would grovel and crawl.

'Don't go yet,' Vanessa said sharply.

'We won't argue, Vanessa.'

'It isn't my way,' she said, and held his arm. They were very close together. Apart from the red swelling at her neck, there was only beauty in her. Her eyes were huge and compelling.

But she wasn't using her beauty or trying to use her body to persuade him, she was using her mind. He wondered again if she were as clever as she was beautiful. Was she seeing how far he would go? Or was fear driving her mad? Had she killed once, and given herself a lust for blood?

'Let's go,' Dawlish said briskly, 'and stop arguing.'

'Pat, what's in your mind? What makes you want them alive? What do they know about you?'

'I'll tell you,' Dawlish said. 'It's simple.'

He told her; there could be no harm in it.

When he had finished, she said slowly:

'So Gurth Haffmeyer put you on the spot, and you think this Orde made him do it.'

'It could be Orde—if Victor didn't lie. Have you ever heard of a man named Orde?'

She had already said 'No', but he waited with fresh hope because of the expression in her eyes.

'Yes,' she said abruptly. 'Gurth was scared to death of a guy named Orde. I don't know much, but I know that. He would take Orde's orders. Gurth might have testified against you, Pat, because Orde said so.'

'I'll find out,' Dawlish said.

'Pat,' she broke in, 'you had plenty of reason to kill Gurth. You say he testified to a Senate Committee, naming you as a man who'd tried first to buy formulae from him, then naming you as a thief. *Did* you kill him?'

'No,' said Dawlish. He bent down, picked up several pebbles, and tossed them into the sea. They skimmed the surface, ricocheting a long way out, sending tiny splashes upwards. He looked straight into her eyes again. 'I'm after Orde, first and last, but I'm not going to kill unless I have to. Get murder out of your mind, Vanessa.'

'What will happen if you're caught?' she asked abruptly.

'Treason—trial—hanging,' Dawlish said, very deliberately and slowly. 'They couldn't do less. But if I can make Orde or anyone else admit that I was framed—'

He lifted his head suddenly and listened.

He heard a new sound, a long way off; none had reached this inlet before, except the sounds of their own making and of the sea—but this was a motor. He looked towards the road. He didn't alter the tone of his voice, but Vanessa turned and looked in the same direction.

They had never heard a car on that road, and therefore didn't know what it would sound like; but to Dawlish the noise of the engine was no longer like that of a car.

A motor-cycle?

The noise of the engine was very loud.

The two men by the cliff were staring towards the road, the danger from Dawlish momentarily forgotten. But Dawlish turned. He knew where the sound came from, that it was neither car nor motor-cycle.

It came from a motor boat which was approaching from the north.

CHAPTER VI

DAWLISH CUTS HAIR

Vanessa's fingers were tight on Dawlish's hand. He drew her closer to him, then began to move, so that they might stand between the people in the motor-boat and the prisoners. He watched the sea. He knew the danger, sensed that Vanessa was alive to it, was aquiver because of it. This might be a launch put out to scan the inlets and the bays by the police, who might not be satisfied with searching the road.

The roar became so loud that it was almost deafening.

The gleaming yellow bows of the motor-boat came in sight.

Dawlish took out cigarettes and handed one to Vanessa; her fingers weren't steady when she took it. He struck a match as a man and a boy came in sight, the boy at the tiller and obviously in high delight. The man was middle-aged, had an old T-shirt of pale blue and white stripes, wore a sailor's cap at a jaunty angle, and had a pipe stuck between his teeth. The boat was a trim little outboard.

Dawlish waved.

'Hi, there!' the man called.

'*Hi!*' shrilled the boy.

Vanessa waved and smiled. Two or three gulls dived and climbed with scornful grace above the widening wake of the motor-boat, which was soon past the inlet.

Both man and boy looked round until the last moment. Then the boat disappeared and the gulls with them.

Dawlish turned round.

'With luck, they won't land for several hours. With more luck, when they do land they won't think of us. The sun was shining straight on you, he probably wouldn't see how beautiful you are!'

His voice was almost casual.

'Pat,' she said, 'don't you ever get scared or excited?'

'There's seldom any need.'

'No need!' They started to walk back towards the two men. 'What are you going to do with Victor?'

'Leave him, and telephone Orde.'

She shrugged her shoulders, and dropped his hand. Until that moment they had been walking hand in hand, towards the prisoners. Dawlish watched them, saw that the squat man was looking at him, but Victor knew better; he was looking at Vanessa's face. He was *much* more frightened of Vanessa than of Dawlish. Perhaps he could judge her better than Dawlish; perhaps he knew there was killer instinct in her. Dawlish sensed that too; sensed her desire to kill. Was that to protect him? Or to save herself?

'Does Orde know this spot?' Dawlish asked Victor.

'No.'

'He'd better find it,' Dawlish said. 'I'm going to telephone him and tell him where you are. I'm going to tie one of you to the back and the other to the front of the car, where you can't be seen from the sea. If you get found by anyone else first . . .' He shrugged.

The relief in Victor's eyes was driven out by a different look, almost one of gloating. Dawlish guessed the cause. Found by others and taken to the police, Victor would tell part of the truth—name Vanessa, and describe Dawlish. Then the police would know that Dawlish and Vanessa had been here.

Everything was ready.

In a few minutes Dawlish would finish tying up Victor and the squat man; then he and Vanessa would step into the scarlet car, a Hudson, and start up the narrow road. It was nearly five hours since they had arrived. He hoped to stop at a motor court after getting food, and sleep for another two or three hours, then drive through the night.

'All set, Vanessa?'

'Yes,' she said. 'Everything's ready.'

She sat in the car, waiting. She didn't look round again, and they started off. Now that the wheel was in his hands, and they were heading for the road again, excitement which wasn't far removed from fear began to beat in Dawlish's heart.

The road had seemed steep coming down; it was much worse going up; at times they were in bottom gear and only just crawling. The corners were sharp, nightmarish. If any other traffic were to come down, they wouldn't get past.

They reached the trees, and the easier gradient. Except for the sound of the engine, there was silence. Then suddenly Vanessa stiffened.

'*Look!*' The word was more whisper than shout.

She was staring towards the right of the road. He glanced that way. A black bear, on its hind legs, stood close to the roadside. It looked like a statue, except that it turned its head, and its little bloodshot eyes were running. They turned another corner, and the bear disappeared.

'It would have been better to shoot them,' Vanessa said tonelessly.

It might have been better to shoot them.

Dawlish drove fast, and Vanessa stared straight ahead. They reached a small town, and he slowed down once they passed the city limits, keeping inside the 35-miles-an-hour speed which the notices ordered. He pulled up under the shade of some chestnut trees, and said:

'I don't think we'll both get out here. Shall I bring you a sandwich?'

'You could do.'

'Ham? Beef?'

'Anything, thanks.'

'Just sit there,' he said. 'There are cigarettes in the glove compartment.' He grinned at her, then studied an Esso map of the district and got out.

Six teen-agers, three boys and three girls, dressed exactly alike in blue jeans and T-shirts except for one girl who wore a blouse, were sitting at the soda fountain, eating sundaes or ice-cream. An old woman with flat feet was poking about the shelves, where a few oddments of hardware goods were on show, all the variety that the store had to offer. A girl behind the soda fountain seemed to be in sole charge, but a man appeared in a doorway near the drug counter.

Dawlish went into the telephone booth, and studied the directions on how to make a call. He called the exchange and gave the number he wanted. Then he put his money in.

The lumber mill was nearly five hundred miles away, and he was speaking to a man there in one minute and thirty seconds.

The man had a deep, heavily accented voice.

'No, Mr. Orde he iss not here.'

'Are you sure?' Dawlish asked. 'This is Dawlish.'

'Dat iss *who*, you say?'

'Dawlish.'

'But I tell you, no, he iss not here!' Something of his emotions showed in the man's voice. 'Dat is—Patrick—'

'Yes. Tell Orde I want to talk to him, soon. Tell him that Victor and the man with him are on a beach at . . .' Dawlish gave details carefully, using the Esso map; Orde—or rather, his agent—had only to get one like it and he would spot the cove in a moment. 'Don't leave them long,' Dawlish said, and rang off.

He stepped out of the box.

The man had come forward from the drug counter, a smiling man in white coat.

'Something I can get for you, sir?'

Dawlish looked at him with his eyes narrowed, and then said, 'Naw,' and shut his mouth. The man said, 'Okay, just look around, it's a pleasure,' and went off. Dawlish searched the shelves, it would have been much quicker to ask for what he wanted but it would give his voice away. He had to do something about that 'accent'.

He found a pair of scissors, two caps with large, wide peaks— green for Vanessa, red for himself. He spotted green eyeshields, and added them to the tally. He found some liniment, too, and black hair-dye. Then he went to the soda fountain, and grunted:

'Two ham.'

'Okay.'

Dawlish studied the colourful advertisements stuck on the mirror, and then a child came in, and soon went off with a chocolate ice-cream on a stick.

'Two,' Dawlish said, and pointed to the child. He grinned.

'Sure, okay.'

He paid; the stuff was wrapped in one parcel. He went out,

the man from the drug counter opening the door. The man disappeared immediately, and Dawlish walked away from the car, then passed the drugstore again and looked in. The man was not at a telephone, but lounging against the soda fountain, unsuspicious.

Vanessa was still sitting in the car.

Solemnly, Dawlish took the silver paper off an ice-cream and held the stick towards her. Her lips relaxed, she smiled and then began to laugh. Dawlish slid in beside her. Solemnly, they ate ice-cream, and, when that was finished, the sandwiches.

He unwrapped the other goods.

'You've bought everything,' Vanessa said.

'Even the scissors. I don't think I'm a good barber but I'll have to try. Ready to move?'

'Sure.'

He drove through the town, turned off to the sea at the first opportunity, then drove off the road, which was of dirt but wider than that which they had used, and pulled up under the trees. Birds flitted through the branches, mosquitoes and insects were humming, dragonflies hovered. The sun found its way with golden brightness through the tops of the trees, but it was cool.

Fifty miles back along the road, a yachtsman and a boy were talking to a motor-cycle cop.

'Sure, there were four, a woman and three men. It was the woman's hair that made me think. The colour!'

'A black Mercury and a red car. Don't you know the name of the red car?'

'I just know it was red,' the yachtsman said.

There had been some felling in the woods where Dawlish and Vanessa were, within the past few years. Once they were beyond the trees which lined the road, they were among tree-trunks which had been taken off smoothly. Dawlish selected one near a shaft of sunlight. He fought back fears—but they were there. A chance visitor to the cove, a mischance of any kind, could be fatal. He needed a spell when he need not be alert every moment.

'Sit there,' he said.

'I don't want hair down my neck,' Vanessa protested.

'I'll get a towel for your shoulders.' Dawlish moved to the back of the car, opened her valise and took out a towel. When he turned towards Vanessa again, she was sitting on the tree trunk, but she had slipped her dress off her shoulders. It fell about her waist, and her skirt was still in position. She wore a white nylon brassiere, so nearly transparent that it hardly mattered.

She looked round at him, her lips parted.

He wrapped the towel round her shoulders.

'Does your neck hurt much?' he asked.

'It's stiff.'

'I'll massage it,' Dawlish promised. 'After I've been a court hairdresser.' He took the scissors and began to snip the hair. It was like committing a crime. The locks weighed heavy, and their auburn had a lustre which was all its own. Soon they made a half-circle about the tree-stump.

Vanessa sat without moving.

Strands and locks fell to the white towel and then gently to the ground. He kept clipping. There had been strange times when he had been barber to his friends; and afterwards they had cut his hair.

As he cut, the hair remaining seemed to curl up defensively. When he finished, it wasn't good but it did not look too bad.

He handed her a mirror.

Then he poured the lotion into his hand, and began to massage her neck, gently. The towel slipped. She didn't look up at him, but straight ahead, towards the distant trees. He kept massaging, with slow, easy movement, as if he would never tire.

She closed her eyes.

The towel slipped to her knees.

When he had finished, and stood back, she looked up at him, through her lashes. She didn't speak, yet seemed to command him to go nearer. He smiled crookedly, and obeyed the command. He stood in front of her, and she stood up quickly, almost savagely. Her arms slid over his shoulders, her body pressed against his.

He kissed her fiercely.

He kissed her again, until she gasped for breath.

He said calmly: 'I'm going back to that inlet, Vanessa. Not down the road, but to the cliff overlooking it. Then we'll see what happens, and how long Orde takes to get busy. You can come, or you can wait for me.'

He had to trust her now.

'I'll come,' she said.

The scarlet Hudson was drawn up off the road, although they hadn't been able to drive far into the forest. They walked together, hands touching, Dawlish with a gun in his righthand pocket. They scanned the clearings for bears, but saw none. Walking towards the cliff didn't take so long as they expected; the sea beckoned them from between the tall trees, and soon they were at the edge. There was just room to walk. Here and there they had to go among the trees, for the sandstone crumbled away; sea and rocks were waiting, two hundred feet below.

A hundred yards to the right, they reached a spot from which they could see the black Mercury and the two men. No one else was there. Neither man was moving; it was possible to believe that they were asleep.

Then Victor stirred.

Dawlish lit a cigarette, and gave it to Vanessa, then lit one himself. He squatted and watched—and she sat on the fallen trunk of a tree, looking at him. Now and again he turned to look at her.

'What do you think of?' she asked.

'Orde.'

'And what else?'

He grinned. 'Nothing.'

'I'll make you think of something else!'

'When I've got Orde, he may give me something else to think of,' Dawlish said. 'Until then, he's all I can think about. Don't let me fool you into getting any other idea.' His grin broadened as he looked into her eyes. Instead of being angry, because he had left the men, she was laughing at him—or with him. His grin faded into an amused smile. He began to run his forefinger down his nose, massaging the broad, broken bridge slightly.

'You and I could get along. Don't do anything I tell you not to, will you?'

'I might,' Vanessa said. 'I might not.'

'Have you ever tried teaching anyone how to speak American?'

She was puzzled; the question drove away the other thoughts in her mind.

'I don't understand you.'

'I have to learn how,' Dawlish said. 'It's partly accent, partly intonation and partly phrasing. I want to learn to speak like a native. You—I mean all of you—have a way of saying "Hi", and I haven't got it yet. Say "Hi".'

Her eyes glowed.

'Hi, Pat.' The short word came slowly, as if she had plenty of time to say it. 'Hi,' she repeated.

'That's fine.' Dawlish said it after her, 'Hi, Vanessa.' He looked his question.

'What's your hurry?' she asked.

'You've spotted the trouble,' he said. 'I'm in too much of a hurry with words. Say some simple things, Vanessa. Just slowly and naturally, don't exaggerate anything.'

'All right,' she said. 'I guess it's time to eat, I'm getting hungry.'

'I guess it's time—'

They played the game for half an hour; she was as enthusiastic as Dawlish by the time he decided that they had had enough for the first lesson. He had eased her tension, too, she wasn't always looking over her shoulder now.

'But whenever I pronounce a word wrongly, tell me,' he said. 'From now on, I'm speaking your language.'

'It's an awful waste of yours,' she said.

Then she saw that he was no longer really with her. He was listening intently. She sat quite still. After a while, a sound travelled to her ears. She looked at him, with a kind of wonderment.

'You belong out here,' she said. 'No Indian could have quicker ears than you.'

It was a car.

The sound was deep and muffled, as if the car were moving between walls; and the only walls they knew of there were the cliffs leading down to the inlet. They watched. The sun was low in the west now, and shining straight into the inlet, turning the yellow sandstone of the cliffs to gold, painting the trees, drawing some of the colour out of the sea. There were the lapping waves and the sparkling diamonds—and the car and the two bound men.

Another car came in sight.

It was a yellow allweather hack, with several police in it.

*   *   *

'So now they'll talk,' Vanessa said; 'we ought to have killed—'

'You're crazy!' Dawlish said roughly. 'The police would have found bodies and more reason for wanting us. Let's move.' They shifted further from the edge, while the police swarmed about Victor and the other man. The sound of voices floated up.

'We must get away,' Vanessa said huskily. All her fear was back.

'Not yet,' Dawlish said. 'Not until they've gone. This is the last place they'll think of looking. They'll expect us to be a hundred miles south.'

Vanessa didn't speak.

'So we wait until it's dark,' Dawlish said.

But the fear remained in her.

Below, the police were talking to Victor. Was he naming Dawlish? Or Orde? Or the lumber camp?

There was no way of telling.

Dawlish looked towards the road leading into the cove—and saw a movement. A yellow convertible appeared, travelling slowly; it stopped. A man got out and walked slowly forward, reached a spot from which he could see the police, waited for a moment, and then darted back to his car.

Soon, he was driving back, up the dirt road towards the highway.

'Come on!' breathed Dawlish.

CHAPTER VII

DEATH ON THE ROAD

They hurried towards the road. A few yards from it, hidden by the trunks of trees, they watched the traffic, hearing the yellow car coming noisily up the dirt road from the inlet. Three cars passed while it was coming up. Then they heard the engine run more smoothly; so it had reached level ground.

It came in sight.

'An Oregon licence,' Vanessa breathed.

Dawlish read the number: 'TOJ561.' The car, still gathering speed, passed slowly, but its pace quickened as it headed towards the south.

They went back to the Hudson and were on the road within ten minutes. Dawlish put his foot down for the first time since they had travelled together. Vanessa sat tensely. They passed four cars, and were still not in sight of the yellow car.

Then they caught up with it, crawling behind a truck with several other cars also dawdling. The cars Dawlish had passed soon drew near. The winding road made it impossible for any car to pass, until the truck turned off where the road was very wide. The rest streamed past quickly, leaving Dawlish within one car of the yellow roadster.

Its driver was a young man, wearing a suit so light that it was almost white. He was bare-headed, and curly yellow hair waved in the wind. He seemed satisfied to lie behind the car ahead; it was keeping a fair speed. They passed through one small town, and reached another, passing many motor-courts and gas stations before they reached the official city limits; this was a larger place.

The driver of the yellow roadster pulled in at a restaurant—the *Golden Shoe.*

Dawlish passed, and saw him clearly—tall, clean-cut, handsome. Then he went inside the restaurant. Dawlish jammed on the brakes, jumped out, and hurried towards the window. There were Venetian blinds, but he could see inside; the fair-headed young man was at the telephone.

He came out of the box, took a table and began to look at the menu.

Dawlish returned to the red Hudson.

'We'll stay around—'

'*Stick* around.'

Dawlish grinned. 'Thanks. We'll stick around for a while. This is probably your lucky place, where we can have a meal that won't leave you hungry.'

'Pat,' she said, and gripped his hand, 'you're crazy. You ought to get a thousand miles away. You haven't a chance to make out. We could drive day and night and be in Mexico in two days—and we wouldn't have another thing to worry about.'

Dawlish said: 'This is my way, Vanessa. I want to put this car out of sight. He might recognize it as Victor's, and the police might know of it. We could trade it.'

'You surely *are* crazy!'

'That's right. We can talk about your idea later. Just now, I say we have to take risks, and the bolder we are the safer we'll be.'

She didn't speak.

He helped her out. There was a smaller restaurant almost opposite the one into which the young man had gone.

'You go and have a wash, and don't put on any lipstick,' Dawlish said. 'Lipstick makes a difference. No one who's heard the radio description of Vanessa Haffmeyer would believe that she would go without any. I won't be long.' He watched her turn into the restaurant, and then drove to the nearest garage—not a gas station, he wanted something bigger. Several cars were outside; one was being greased, another washed.

A brisk man with spotless white shirt and a spotted bow tie came forward.

'I don't know if you can help me,' Dawlish said, 'I'm having trouble with the car, I don't know what it is. I can't afford to buy another. If I leave this one with you for repair, can you hire me one for a few days?'

'Why, sure, sure!'

'One I can rely on,' said Dawlish.

'I wouldn't rent a car that wasn't one hundred per cent good,' the young man said. He grinned. 'And you're coming back, I guess!'

Ten minutes later, Dawlish drew up outside the smaller restaurant in a powder-blue Chevrolet with a big vizor which shaded the passengers and turned their faces greeny-blue. The engine seemed to turn over sweetly. He went in; Vanessa wasn't there. He had a wash in the rest-room, and when he came out Vanessa had taken a window seat. She still wore her peaked cap, at an angle; it was almost possible to see her as a different woman. Few were likely to recognize her from the radio description. But soon there would be newspapers with her photograph in it, and the police were experts at identifying faces from photographs.

He joined her.

'I've ordered steaks and French fried,' she said.

They finished the meal with coffee and an ice-cream. The man in the yellow convertible didn't come out. Dawlish began to feel on edge.

Vanessa said, 'He's having himself quite a meal.'

'I hope so,' Dawlish said. 'Stay for five minutes, then go to the car.'

She nodded.

Dawlish went out, paying the bill at the cashier's desk, and taking two packs of Pall Mall, and several books of matches. The woman at the desk had dyed black hair and a very white face. Her eyes were almost black. She looked at him from under her lashes, and he sensed that she was staring after him.

He moved along by the window, outside.

There was a telephone by the side of the cashier. There was no way to stop her from lifting it, calling the police, reporting that she had seen the big man with the fair hair. His hair ought to be dyed while he was in the open, like this.

She did not appear to touch the telephone.

Vanessa looked a question—but he didn't try to answer by dumb play. He crossed the road. The window of the larger restaurant was screened with net curtains. He went in. It was very cool, and air-conditioning machines were buzzing. It was an exclusive place, with red leather chairs and classy tables and pictures of blondes and brunettes in various stages of undress round the walls. Half a dozen people sat at the tables; half a dozen waiters in white stood about. There was a cocktail bar but no soda fountain.

The fair-haired man wasn't in sight.

Dawlish strolled towards the bar, sat on a stool, lit a cigarette and looked into the barman's plump face.

'What's yours, sir?'

'John Collins,' Dawlish said. He could use the accent for that; and no one would expect him to talk much. He watched the man mix the drink—and, in a mirror, watched a door marked *Manager.* It remained closed while he sipped his drink and smoked.

Two or three more customers came in.

He lit another cigarette and repeated the order, paid for it, and then over the barman's shoulder saw the door open. The tall, fair-haired man came out. His reflection didn't give the slightest suggestion that he was a killer; in fact, he looked a nice boy. He wasn't alone; a stocky man in a biscuit-coloured shirt, yellow-and-black bow tie and thin black hair, was with him—an oozing type.

'Sure, Johnny, you've done fine, fine. Don't you worry at all. Just you go home and wait, don't worry at all. We'll fix everything.' He had a diamond solitaire ring on the hand with which he patted the youth's shoulder. 'Don't you worry.'

'Why should I worry?' Johnny grinned at him. Neither of them appeared to notice Dawlish, who hunched his shouldders, to make himself look smaller than he was.

Johnny went out.

The door swung to.

Dawlish finished his drink, and was at the door when the stocky man had disappeared into his office. Outside, the fair-haired youth was strolling towards his convertible. Across the road, the door of the other restaurant opened, and Vanessa appeared.

She went towards the blue Chevrolet.

Johnny climbed into the yellow convertible.

Vanessa got into the Chevrolet and started the engine.

'Do you want to follow him?'

'How did you guess?'

'I've been thinking about you,' she said. She turned the car until it faced the same direction as the convertible. The fair-haired youth was already moving along the road—southwards. He passed. He didn't glance at them, seemed to concentrate on the road. A mile out of town, he began to travel fast. Dawlish saw his own speedometer touching eighty, and didn't think that the Chevrolet could do much more in comfort.

The convertible was a hundred yards ahead, just a yellow streak when it turned a corner.

They turned it, also.

They were in time to see the convertible swing off the road. It happened in a flash of time. One moment it was moving steadily, smoothly; the next it went out of control. At that speed, any crash was bound to be disastrous, and it was more disastrous because another car was hurtling towards it. Even before it happened, when Dawlish knew that the smash was inevitable, it was hideous.

Then came the smash. The yellow convertible seemed to buckle like tin-foil, and the other car leapt over it. Both went on their sides. The noise was hideous, too, as if metal were screaming a protest for the flesh and bones which were being mashed and mangled.

Vanessa trod on the brake.

There was just room to pass, and just time to stop before reaching the two wrecked cars. Both had stopped moving, except for quivering—and no fire had started.

'Pass them,' Dawlish said. 'Step on it!'

Vanessa reacted quickly. Next moment, they flashed past; and Dawlish caught a sight of the man's fair hair, untouched with blood; oddly, he was still sitting at the wheel. From the chin up he looked quite normal, except that his eyes were closed.

'Faster!'

Vanessa obeyed. Dawlish looked round. No other car was coming from either direction.

They turned a corner.

'It may have been an accident, or the convertible might have been fixed to go out of control,' Dawlish said. 'We can't argue about that. We can about other things, Vanessa.'

'I can find plenty to argue about,' she said bitterly. 'If you'd killed Victor—'

'Forget it.' Dawlish was driving now, looking straight ahead. 'The police know we're together. We'd be safer apart.'

She didn't speak.

'Wouldn't we?' he insisted.

'Is that your way of giving me the brush-off?'

He knew that she was looking at him angrily.

'It's my way of saying that if you don't like the things I do, you needn't stay,' Dawlish said. 'You want to ride for Mexico. I don't. I've a hope of getting myself cleared—you don't seem to think you've a chance. Did you kill Haffmeyer?'

'No!' She almost shouted at him. 'But they'll hang it on to me.'

Dawlish said: 'If you'll play this my way, we can keep together. But it must be my way.'

'Pat,' she said, 'Victor probably told the police about Orde. Even if you get to the lumber camp, Orde won't be there.'

'I think he will. I don't think Victor will tell the police a thing,' Dawlish said. 'He told us what he did because he was scared we'd kill him—he won't feel that way about the police.'

She didn't speak for a while. Then:

'I don't want to go my own way,' she said. 'I'll take a chance with you.'

* * *

But she would try again, he knew.

Why did she want to stay with him? Did she fear being too frightened on her own?

Dawlish put that out of his mind. Glancing at her, he marvelled again at her beauty. There could not be many as beautiful, few who came near her.

He thought of his own wife—Felicity.

Felicity knew what he was doing. She was frightened, because she knew of the dread consequences of failure. They had said little when he had crept out of London; but fear had been in her mind and knowledge of it in his. She was not beautiful, as Vanessa was beautiful, but to him she was everything.

Yet he had to put this chase first.

He had to work as if he were not married; as if he could not even think of the past, only of the future. He had to be utterly single-minded. If Vanessa could help him to get what he wanted, he would have to use Vanessa; and there was nothing, no way at all, in which he would not use her.

He believed she could be deadly.

She had been badly upset by the road accident. Why?

There was plenty to think about.

He'd had the luck with the police—so much that he was feeling puzzled. Were the police really trying? At the back of his mind, he doubted it. Look at it straight, and what did one see? He was named as a traitor and there was much evidence against him, for others besides Haffmeyer had testified to his villainy. So the police knew—or believed—that he was a traitor. So did the British and the American secret services. They would want to know whom he served—to whom he sold the information he was believed to have stolen. So, they might have him watched without taking action until they believed he had led them to the King-pin.

That was how he would play such a hand.

That was how they were playing it; he felt sure of this in his bones—and yet he might be wrong. Even if danger from the police was being held back, danger from Orde wasn't. Orde wanted to kill him. . . .

Who had killed Haffmeyer?

Vanessa?

Or Orde's men, for fear Haffmeyer would talk to Dawlish?

There was no way of telling—yet.

There was no way of being sure that when he got to the lumber camp Orde would be there—but he could hope, and if needs be go on from there.

The lumber mill was still nearly five hundred miles away.

He could not make up his mind whether to stay on this road or to go inland. There was no doubt that the whole of the district was being watched. He needed to escape observation, even if the police were trailing him but keeping off. He wanted to reach the camp unseen.

Vanessa broke his chain of thought.

'Pat.'

'Hallo?'

'Is that right, you're married?'

'Yes.'

'What's she like? Beautiful?'

Dawlish didn't take his eyes off the road. He could say that to him Felicity had all the beauty of women. He could say that there was really one woman, and only one, and there would never be another. Vanessa might believe him. He didn't want her to believe that. He wasn't sure of how he would be able to use her, or what was in her mind; but he was quite sure that it would be wise to let her think that she could make a conquest, even if she hadn't yet.

So he looked at her, suddenly, swiftly, and grinned.

'Why should you care?' he said.

The look in her amber eyes made him think it was what she wanted to hear.

CHAPTER VIII

SITTING BIRD

It was dark.

Dawlish lay on his bed, looking at the window. There were lights outside the motel—some of them flashing on and off, but none close enough to dazzle, or be a nuisance.

Vanessa lay on the bed next to him, asleep.

She was very beautiful. . . .

They had been here for six hours; had come soon after she had asked him about Felicity and, in a way, he had lied. He found himself smiling faintly in the darkness. The simple truth was that Vanessa had been *tired;* more tired than he had realized, much more tired than he. He had seen that when they had come in.

He had left her for ten minutes, to undress. When he had come back, she had been in bed, drowsy, yet waiting for him.

'What are you going to do, Pat?'

'Sleep well,' he said.

She hadn't answered; just smiled.

Now, he was awake. He couldn't be sure of the time, but he guessed that it would soon be dawn.

He pushed the clothes back and got up, went into the shower, stripped, and was glad of the cool water. He rubbed himself down gently, then stepped into the room and pulled on his clothes. She did not appear to wake up. He lit a cigarette, then went outside. Cars whined past, headlights blazing. He looked towards the eastern sky, and saw the first hint of dawn; a lovely dawn, all days seemed to be the same here, and the morning and the evening were perfect.

The neon lights were at gas stations and all-night restaurants, a hot-dog stand. He went to the stand and had coffee, served by a girl who looked as if she hadn't been to sleep for days.

He went back to the motel.

Vanessa was awake. He saw the glitter of her eyes, but she kept quite still. He closed the door behind him, and looked at her.

'Sleep well?' he asked.

She didn't pretend any longer.

'So you haven't run out on me.'

'Not yet,' he said. 'We've a lot to do together. I think we can say that we need each other.' He sat down, massive and handsome, on his own bed and ran his fingers through his hair. 'You look just fine. Remember that gun you had when you first interrupted me?'

The smile which curved her lips disappeared; in a moment she was wary.

'What if I do?'

'Ever used it to shoot with?'

She looked at him searchingly, and then her smile came back. She nodded. In a way, Dawlish thought, her bobbed hair made her look younger, took the sophistication out of her beauty. The colour was glorious, and the electric light caught it at exactly the right angle. Her shoulders were bare. Her throat was flawless, like her skin.

'Yes,' she said. 'I learned to look after myself.'

'When—and why?'

'I was brought up the hard way,' she said. 'And when I married Gurth, he knew that there might be trouble any time. He taught me how to shoot. And I can shoot!'

She said it in such a way that he was sure that she could; she did more—impressed him with the feeling that she had used a gun before, that it didn't matter much to her. He found himself wondering again whether she had killed—and then, how many she had killed. His curiosity about her would flame into life if he let it; so for the time being he had to control curiosity. He wanted to learn the truth about her gradually; to form a picture which could come out of little things she did and said, the unconsidered, careless trifles.

'That's fine,' he said.

'Why?' When he didn't answer, she went on, 'I thought you disapproved of me shooting anyone.'

'It depends on the circumstances, sweetheart.' He lit a cigarette, leaned forward, and held it to her lips. She took it. She had been so tired the night before that the contrast of her freshness now was remarkable. Her beauty held that touch of innocence again.

'What's on your mind?' she asked.

'I want to send Orde a message he won't forget. I want to make him think it's worth playing with me, listening to me. I'm going to find out how he's thinking now, so I'm going to tell him that I'll be at a certain place at a certain time.'

She said, suddenly hard-voiced, 'And then?'

'You're going to cover me with the gun. If any man Orde sends tries any funny business, then you can shoot.'

'You'd trust yourself to me as far as that?'

Dawlish grinned. 'Show me what choice I have,' he said. 'Show me anyone else I can trust.' he moved suddenly, seized

75

her shoulders, drew her up from the pillows, and kissed her lips until it hurt. 'I'll trust you,' he growled. 'And if you frame me, I'll find a way of making the police believe that you killed Gurth. They'd be tickled pink to find his killer.'

She looked up at him, her eyes glowing.

'I won't frame you,' she said.

There was a small restaurant nearby, where half an hour later they had breakfast. They were the only customers. A flat-chested, flabby-looking girl served them with bacon and eggs and wheatcakes with maple syrup; then she went away and gazed dreamily at a juke box which was emitting a shrill male voice.

Vanessa looked rested; younger; eager to please. In fact she looked wonderful.

'Pat,' she said. 'Are you sure it's a good thing to let Orde know where you are?'

'I want to talk to him,' Dawlish said. 'I want to make him think it's worth playing ball with me. I've worked for the British Government a hell of along time. There's a lot Orde would like to know—and he can be made to realize it. If he thinks that I'll talk, perhaps he'll stop the shooting war.'

'But after you've talked, he'll cut your throat.'

Dawlish said: 'It's a big throat. I have a lot of ideas, too, Vanessa, and Orde might be interested in some of them. I'm going to telephone him again.'

He went to the telephone in a corner. Vanessa watched, sipping her coffee, then lighting a cigarette. He dialled, and then gave the number of the lumber camp. This time the call took three minutes to come through, although he was a hundred miles nearer.

The man with the heavily accented voice spoke.

'This is Dawlish,' Dawlish said, 'and I want to talk to Orde.'

As he spoke, the risks seemed to snarl at him; there was even a risk that the operator would recognize his English voice, and would report to the police. He didn't know how far the police search had gone, couldn't be sure they were stalling. He hadn't seen a newspaper, and ought to find out as soon as possible whether there was a picture of him in a newspaper; or of Vanessa.

There was sure to be one of Vanessa.

The man gasped, 'Did you say—'

'That's what I said, and I don't want to say it again. Put Orde on the line.'

'Wait—wait joost a minute!'

'Make it quick.'

A motor-cycle passed outside. Dawlish saw Vanessa's eyes turned towards the window, and looked out himself. The rider was a cop.

He could imagine Vanessa's heart thumping.

He put the thought out of his mind.

A man said: 'So that's *Pat*rick. This is Orde.'

It was a strange voice, rather high-pitched, almost musical; a voice which was easy to identify. Somehow, it wasn't quite a human voice—more like one which came out of a juke box or the radio.

'Listen,' Dawlish said, 'I'll be at the *Silver Slipper* restaurant at Wyma, all day. I want to talk to you. That's as good a place as any.'

'But, *Pat*rick—' There was mockery in the voice.

'I'll be there in two hours,' Dawlish said. 'And I'll stay for just one day. I can tell you a lot in one day—if it's worth good money to you.'

He rang off.

The girl who had served them was still staring dreamily at the juke box, although it had stopped playing. Vanessa slid off her stool. Dawlish picked up the bill, laid the money on the counter with a quarter tip and went out.

'What did he say?' asked Vanessa.

'It's what he's going to do that counts,' Dawlish said.

The thing that mattered—at times he thought it was the only thing that mattered—was talking to Orde, persuading Orde to listen to him, giving himself a chance to find out just why Orde had branded him, and getting proof that he was innocent. Dawlish did not let himself think further than that; in fact he thought little further than the *Silver Slipper*. He had picked the name of the place out of a folder which had been on the counter of a restaurant. It would probably be a big one. He drove towards Wyma with Vanessa at his side. Looking out for it caused him no bother. The restaurant was by the city limits, and above the roof of a log-walled building was a huge silver slipper which glistened in the rising sun. As they drew closer, other slippers showed up— at the windows, the chimneys, on finger posts pointing towards it. There was kerb service, and two cars were waiting for it.

Dawlish drove straight through the town; and then turned back at the first opportunity.

It was two hours since they had telephoned Orde. Orde wouldn't come himself; he couldn't, anyway. Everything depended on whether he had an envoy near; whether he would send one to talk, or whether he still meant to kill.

He pulled up at a petrol station near the *Silver Slipper*, where there was an open space close to the road. The day was already warming up. Traffic was much thicker now, too. A huge truck went by, hauling lumber—great tree-trunks which looked fantastically big. It went out of sight.

'If Orde is sending someone from the lumber camp, he won't arrive for several hours,' Dawlish said. 'If he's sending an agent who lives near here, the agent might arrive any time.'

'Pat,' Vanessa said, and took his hands. 'Listen to me. The best way out would be to disappear. You could forget the whole bad business. We have money, haven't we? Orde isn't likely to let you get away with anything. You stand to lose everything and win nothing. Let's drive on.'

Dawlish grinned. 'Mexico calling? Go on your own, or wait with me for this party. You sit in the car, sweetheart. I'll take a walk.' He looked down at her handbag; the gun was inside. 'Don't use it unless you have to.'

'You're still crazy,' she said. Her eyes blazed.

He knew that he was; that he was following a hunch. He had often followed hunches, and lived through them; but he had never struck anything quite so vicious, quite so deadly. It showed in his nerves. He waited his chance and crossed the road and stood by the *Silver Slipper*. People looked at him but no one spoke, no one took any real interest. The worst of this, as well as the worst of anything, was the waiting.

It might have to be for hours.

In fact it was for two hours and forty minutes. At the end of the time, he was hot, and Vanessa looked hotter. At the end of the time, people at the *Silver Slipper* and at the nearby gas station had forgotten to take any more notice of him—they seemed to regard him as a fixture.

A car came from the north.

It was hard to say why Dawlish watched it more closely than all the others; perhaps because it slowed down. Others had, also, because of the restaurant sign, but this one—there seemed to be something different about it. A man sat next to the driver, too; a man in a pink shirt. He seemed to be watching. He *was* watching. No one else was on the road, no one was in sight. At fifty yards the car was almost at a standstill. The man spoke to the driver—and next moment Dawlish saw the gun in his hand and knew Orde's answer.

CHAPTER IX

QUICK SHOOTING

Dawlish leapt.

He was close to the corner of the *Silver Slipper*, and reached its cover as he heard the bark of a shot. He saw a girl standing just inside the restaurant look up sharply. Another shot came. Both bullets smacked into the wooden walls. Then he heard a third shot.

He came up against the wall, out of range now, and saw Vanessa. She sat in the Chevrolet with the door open. He saw the gun in her hand with smoke rising from it. The attacker car was a long way off, and going faster. So the attack had come and Vanessa had kept her word.

Behind him a man said, 'Don't move, mister.'

That was all.

Vanessa, across the road, dropped the gun into her bag. She smiled across at Dawlish, who was near the corner and in sight—but the man behind him wasn't in view of Vanessa.

'Just don't move,' the man repeated.

Dawlish didn't even look round; but out of the corner of his eyes he saw the reflection of a short man in a mirror. He saw hands move. He knew that he might be killed in that instant; that a knife could do its vicious work swiftly, silently.

The man wasn't yet within reach of his heel—back-heeling was his only means of defence. He opened his mouth as if shouting, but no sound came—it was a silent signal to Vanessa. He mouthed the shout again.

She frowned, puzzled.

The man said; 'If you try anything, Dawlish, you'll get your trouble from the gas station. See the guy in a red shirt?'

A tall, thin man in a red shirt lounged by the wall of the gas station on the other side of the road. He moved slowly. He looked across at Dawlish but in fact he was getting nearer the Chevrolet. Now and again he glanced at Vanessa; but Vanessa had eyes only for Dawlish.

She got out of the car. Her long legs looked sleek and seductive.

A hand touched Dawlish.

The fear of death, so close until that moment, faded slightly. Would they do all this if they intended to kill? He felt the hand at his pockets, round his waist, beneath his arms. The man touched the gun in his right coat pocket and drew it out. The way he transferred it from Dawlish's pocket to his own was almost sleight-of-hand.

'We're going to cross the road,' the man said. 'Don't make any mistakes.' He smiled. 'And then we're going for a ride.'

The old phrase, that hackneyed old phrase, suddenly became aflame with meaning; and with menace. The danger hadn't passed, had simply been suspended.

'Just walk,' the man said.

Something hard pressed into the small of Dawlish's back. It might be a gun; it might be anything. He glanced at the window again. He couldn't see what it was. He saw the backs of two or three girls, waitresses in pink dresses, at the main window overlooking the road. They probably thought they'd heard a car back-firing. They were watching Vanessa and the man in the red shirt.

'Get moving,' the man ordered.

Dawlish moved slowly forward. Cars kept passing, some of them doing eighty or ninety miles an hour. Another of the huge lumber trucks passed—carrying a tree so big that it seemed unreal. Dawlish noticed it without thinking of anything except the 'something' pressing into his back.

They stood close together by the verge of the road. The man with the gun, if it were a gun, was almost level with Dawlish, and the pressure was now in Dawlish's side. As car after car hurtled past, they waited.

Then came another lull in the traffic.

'Get moving,' the man said again.

Across the road, Vanessa was by the side of the car and staring about her; suddenly, she turned to one side, as if she were no longer interested. The man in the red shirt would know in a flash if she tried to help, but she might not know about him. Dawlish prayed that she wouldn't try anything, because in giving him a chance she would certainly die.

She went back to the car.

The man in the red shirt had black hair, and black stubble was like a rash on his cheeks and chin. He didn't look at Vanessa again, but went to a green Buick parked by the side of the gas station.

He was at the wheel and driving closer to the road, when Dawlish and the man beside him reached the other side.

'Go over there,' the man said. 'Get in that car—next to the driver.'

Dawlish turned.

If he obeyed, they might really take him for a ride; might? Almost certainly they would. He wouldn't have a chance once they reached the journey's end. If Orde wanted to hear what he had to say, they would have used different tactics. If he put up a fight now, would he win his chance to live? There was nothing to stop them from shooting him and getting away.

Judging the right moment to fight was supremely important. It had to be the one moment when they weren't expecting trouble.

He went closer to the car, walking slowly, reluctantly.

He wanted desperately to see Orde, and might conceivably have a chance to persuade them that they ought to let him. He could try.

'Inside,' the man said, in a soft voice.

If he were going to fight, this was the moment when they would expect trouble and be ready for him. From now on their alertness would slacken—slightly, but definitely. A rush for illusory safety now would put him on the ground with a bullet in his vitals.

He heard another engine start up.

Vanessa was driving the Chevrolet off in the opposite direction.

Dawlish put a foot inside the gunman's car. Sweat was hot on his forehead and the back of his neck, and made his clothes cling to him. He couldn't see Vanessa, because she was travelling in the other direction; away from them, away from the direction in which this car was pointing. Why? Had fear driven her?

The 'thing' poked into his ribs again, painfully.

He climbed in, next to the man in the red shirt. The other got in the back. For the first time Dawlish turned to look at him. He was a small man, with a flabby face and nasty, bulging little eyes. He had a big, floppy jowl and a small mouth. His hair was turning grey, and was plastered all over a turnip-shaped head.

He showed an automatic pistol; so that hadn't been bluff.

'Okay, Joe,' he said. His voice reminded Dawlish of a sponge.

The driver waited for his chance, and slid on to the road. He put his foot down. They moved fast; and it looked to Dawlish as if they knew exactly where they were going and what they wanted to do. The man with the floppy jowl sat on the edge of his seat, and his breath was warm and unpleasant on the back of Dawlish's neck.

The speedometer needle touched seventy.

Dawlish said, 'I told Orde—'

'Shut your can,' the man behind him said.

'I want to see—'

'I told you,' the man said. He clouted Dawlish on the side of the head with the muzzle of the gun. It was painful, but it wasn't the pain which affected Dawlish—it was the casual callousness of the action. These were Orde's men; there was good reason to believe that Orde was a killer who played for high stakes. He would use the kind of men who could kill, would kill, without the slightest compunction.

They were travelling faster.

Dawlish said, 'Orde must like trouble.'

He expected another blow; his muscles were stiff as he prepared to resist it—to fight against the pain. The certain thing was that he couldn't make a move to help himself. He might be able to when they slowed down, but there would be no certainty.

The man said, 'Orde *never* gets trouble.'

'If Orde doesn't talk to me, he'll throw away a million dollars,' Dawlish said.

Would that impress them? He had let himself be held, taken a desperate chance, to convince Orde of the need to see him—and money should talk.

The man behind Dawlish gave a little giggle; just a nasty little giggle. It affected Dawlish much more than shouted threats would have done, brought disappointment sharply, increased fears. '*Tee-hee-hee,*' the man said, and then added:

'Forget it. You're going to a place where money doesn't count.'

Dawlish felt cold enough to shiver, although it was so hot and there was no air-conditioner in the car. He sat motionless.

A car passed them.

It wasn't until it was swinging in front of them, fifty yards ahead, that he realized that it was Vanessa in the powder-blue Chevrolet. She hadn't glanced at him. She had just put her foot down and passed; they were doing seventy-five.

Vanessa vanished round a bend.

They turned it, and the Chevrolet was too far ahead to be overtaken. They kept up the whining speed.

There was a signpost ahead, and a turning to the right. They slowed down. The man behind Dawlish seemed to draw back; when Dawlish looked round at him, he saw that the gun was covering his head; the man appeared to realize that this was another dangerous moment.

They turned the corner.

Vanessa was some distance ahead.

This was a wide road, with no traffic in sight.

'So Orde really wants trouble,' Dawlish said.

'Orde can look after himself,' the flabby man said. 'Okay, Joe.' As he spoke, he slapped Dawlish across the face with his left hand. Dawlish *knew* what was coming; *knew* that the slap was to tell him that the shooting would start. He flung himself to one side against the driver. He heard the roar of the shot. A hole leapt into the windscreen, then a big white star. The car went out of control.

Dawlish twisted himself round and aimed a sweeping blow at the flabby man, who was reeling backwards as the car swerved, and had lost control of his gun. Dawlish missed his head but it didn't matter. He twisted round, leaned over and grabbed the flabby man's neck. It was like clutching foam rubber. He gripped and shook the man viciously—and the little bulging eyes seemed to come out further; his small pink mouth opened and white teeth and a pinker tongue showed. The man at the wheel was getting control again, Dawlish hadn't long to work. He swung his right arm round and caught the driver a glancing blow as the car jolted to a standstill.

A car appeared alongside.

Vanessa was there; and as the Chevrolet stopped she flung the door open. The driver of Dawlish's car couldn't fail to see the gun in her hand.

The driver actually *screamed*.

Vanessa wanted to kill.

She looked at the driver as she raised the gun, and there was deadliness in her eyes—deadliness and hatred and something which the man recognized and Dawlish recognized, but which was hard to name. Ruthlessness? There was only a second or two in which to act. Dawlish was leaning over the back of the seat, still clutching the flabby man round the flabby neck.

Dawlish let him go, and found his gun. By then Vanessa had opened the door. By then, too, a truck was coming towards them, and Vanessa didn't shoot or speak. Her face was close to

Dawlish, but she was looking at the driver in the red shirt; it was as if her fingers itched to shoot him.

The truck slowed down.

'You want some help?' the driver called. He was little more than a boy.

Vanessa turned. Dawlish could only see her profile, but that was enough to show the transformation; it was hard to believe that she was the same woman. The truck driver looked dazed, dazzled.

'That's very kind of you, but we're fine,' she said. 'My friend got into a skid.'

'Sure, okay,' the truck driver gasped, and stared at her. Then he started violently, and grabbed at the wheel. 'Sure, ma'am, any time!' He nearly stalled the engine as he started off, utterly confused because of the bewildering beauty which had been turned on him like a searchlight.

The flabby man's eyes were closed, and he slumped back in the corner.

Joe, the man in the red shirt, looked at Vanessa as if he were the rabbit and she the stoat.

'Glad to see you, Vanessa,' Dawlish said, as he got out of the car, and tried to make himself sound natural. 'I was expecting a little trouble.' He took out cigarettes; he needed a drink, but a cigarette would have to do. 'Keep them covered.'

He half expected her to shoot them.

She didn't.

'What are you going to do with them?' she asked stonily. 'If you want to know what they would have done with you, I can tell you.'

'They don't count,' Dawlish said. The cigarette smoke had never tasted better. 'The only man who counts is Orde.' He went round to the other side of the car. The flabby man's eyes were open a little; he wasn't unconscious but probably wished he were. 'You're to tell Orde I *must* see him,' Dawlish said. 'I can offer him—'

A shot barked.

The driver, the man in the red shirt, gave a choking cry.

Smoke curled from Vanessa's gun.

CHAPTER X

VICTIM

The driver had been getting out of his seat, and feeling for a gun in a shoulder holster. Now he slumped down—resting against the seat, but with one foot on the dusty road. His right hand was hidden inside the gaping front of his shirt; that red shirt. A leather holster showed—he had been drawing a gun.

Darker red also showed, close to the left breast; the red of blood.

He looked at Vanessa.

As if in a moment of final defiance, he moved his hand further inside his shirt, groping for the gun. Neither Dawlish nor the girl moved. The man's fingers hadn't the strength. His arm fell, and would have fallen to the seat but for the button of the shirt, which held the forearm up. The pallor of his face was worse, and his eyes glittered, as if they were looking upon horror.

He mouthed words at Vanessa.

None was intelligible.

The flabby man sat on the back seat, his eyes wide open and protruding; browny-black eyes. Their gaze darted from Vanessa to Dawlish and back again. He had his hands on his knees, as if to make sure that no one even feared that he would try to get at a gun.

Vanessa said in an unemotional voice, 'He would have shot you.'

'I can believe it,' Dawlish said. This wasn't the moment to worry about Vanessa's trigger-happy fingers, her urge to kill Orde's men. 'We've got to get off the road.' A dozen things needed doing at the same moment, and it would be easy to try to do too many things. 'Park the Chevrolet and come back in a hurry.'

She almost ran to the Chevrolet.

Dawlish opened the rear door of the other car, felt in the flabby man's pockets, found another gun in a shoulder holster and took it away. He didn't say a word. The man was short and plump, with very tight-fitting clothes; his trousers seemed to cling to him. He reminded Dawlish of the manager of the restaurant, who had patted Johnny on the back and sent him out.

'Don't move,' Dawlish said, 'or you'll get hurt too.'

He pushed the driver away from the driving wheel. The man didn't move at all. His eyes were closed now, and his chin drooped to his chest—not far from the patch of dark red which was spreading over the bright red of his shirt. Red on red. Blood on red—the life blood of a man. Dawlish took the wheel, with the dead man leaning against him. By then Vanessa had parked the Chevrolet off the road, and was coming back. She didn't run—probably because a car was approaching. Her expression was despairing. Its driver gave them a casual stare; that was all.

'See that he doesn't try any tricks,' Dawlish said, and jerked his head towards the flabby man.

'Okay.' She climbed into the green Buick, and Dawlish started off.

'See what our guest has in his pockets,' Dawlish added. 'He hasn't a gun but might have a lot of other things.'

Vanessa didn't answer, but he was sure she would obey.

There were trees on either side of the road and no indication, here, as to where the road led. He didn't think that it mattered much. He drove for half a mile, then found a narrow dirt road leading among the trees. He turned into it. Soon, the road led onwards, below road level. Trees had been felled, all about them, and there was plenty of room to drive. Timber trucks had once made the road; it was deeply rutted in places, with hard mud.

Dawlish stopped when they were out of sight of the road. Only birds and insects moved about them.

Dawlish got out.

The dead man lolled towards the driving seat. Blood had spread from the shirt to the trousers and dripped to his knees. His mouth was slack. Dawlish found himself remembering the words he had mouthed, or tried to mouth, but couldn't recall a thing.

Vanessa got out of the car. 'Here's what I found,' she said, quite calmy. 'His name's Klimm—Cyrus Klimm. He doesn't look like a Cyrus to me.'

She handed Dawlish some papers. There were letters, addressed to Cyrus Klimm, manager of the *Silver Slipper*. Dawlish didn't like that—he had selected the *Silver Slipper* simply by chance, and the manager was one of Orde's men. Luck could turn one way or the other, but that kind of luck was fantastically bad; that kind of coincidence almost unbelievable. He read the letters; they said nothing that mattered.

Then Dawlish turned over a postcard, and found that he was looking at a photograph of himself. It did him justice. In fact it flattered him, showing a smile he hadn't felt like giving Vanessa very often, a gleam in his eyes—a face that people would like.

Vanessa took it.

'It's not bad,' she said judicially.

'How did you get this?' Dawlish asked the man.

Until that moment, Cyrus Klimm hadn't uttered a word, had just looked from one to the other, as if trying to anticipate what they wanted him to do, and make sure that there could be no excuse for smacking him down. He closed his eyes before he spoke; and the words came in an earnest voice, comically different from his tone when he had talked to Dawlish before.

'It was sent to me by Mr. Orde.'

'When?'

'Three days ago.'

'Why?'

'Mr. Orde,' said Klimm, very cautiously and carefully, 'gave me to understand that we might have some business together, and that it would be a good thing if I were able to identify you.'

'What kind of business?'

'Mr. Orde didn't say.'

'When did you get later instructions about me?'

'By telephone, this morning.'

'What instructions?'

Klimm blinked, and then looked at Vanessa. His look suggested that he thought Dawlish might believe him, but he was doubtful about her. It was peculiar how they all feared Vanessa—as Victor had, from the beginning. Was it just her expression? Her eyes held that unspoken desire to kill—and the man realized it.

Why did she feel that way?

Nothing in her expression suggested that the prisoner was wrong. He licked his lips, and then said in the same very flat, careful voice:

'I was to frighten you into telling me why you want to see Mr. Orde.'

'Frighten!' Vanessa broke in, sneering. 'You were going to kill him, you weren't going to talk. . . . Why waste time, Pat?'

Dawlish didn't speak, but went through the other papers which she had taken from Klimm's pocket. None of these helped. An alligator-skin wallet was filled with dollar bills—Klimm carried nearly two thousand dollars in all; and a few oddments.

'Is Orde still at the lumber mill?' Dawlish asked.

'Yes.'

'Did Victor name him to the police?'

'I wouldn't know, but Orde telephoned me an hour before we started out. He's still at the camp.'

Dawlish said: 'Tell him I want to see him, because if he's got any sense, we can do a deal. Remind him I've had access to a lot of secret information.'

He turned away.

Vanessa clutched at his arm.

'You're not going to *leave* him free!'

'That's exactly what I'm going to do.' Dawlish forced a grin. It wasn't easy—because she seemed to be saying that she really wanted to kill Klimm as she had killed the man in the red shirt. *Did* she lust for blood? 'Getting his friend away and talking to Orde are his worries. We're leaving.'

He turned and walked towards the road. For a moment, Vanessa stood still. Dawlish felt a sudden surge of alarm, almost of panic. She might kill because she couldn't bring herself to obey him.

He swung round.

She was looking at Klimm.

The terror in the man's eyes had to be seen to be believed; he stood looking at her, as if begging with all his being that she shouldn't shoot him. She had the gun in her hand.

The very way she looked at a man could terrify him.

She turned slowly.

She didn't look at Dawlish, but she handed him the gun. He had a strange feeling—that she had fought and won a battle with herself.

Dawlish lit a cigarette for her while sitting at the wheel of the Chevrolet, and turned the car round and went back to the highway. He turned left—towards the *Silver Slipper* and the towns through which they had once passed. He didn't travel too fast, until he came in sight of the *Silver Slipper*. Then he put his foot down, for a crowd had gathered, two motorcycle cops were pushing their way through it, a siren whined.

Dawlish didn't look to see if anyone took notice, but as they passed, watched the mirror.

No car pulled out to follow them.

But the police had soon been there. The girls in the restaurant would describe him, and perhaps Vanessa.

At least they had a different car. But if the police really wanted them, a net could be spread that they couldn't escape. Were the police playing with them, cat and mouse—waiting for Dawlish to lead them to some unknown hide-out, to accomplices or leaders?

The police were on one side, a constant menace. And Orde was on the other.

Had Klimm lied about his instructions?

Dawlish drove on, still at speed.

'How far back are we going?' Vanessa asked.

'The *Golden Shoe*.'

'Why?'

'There's a man at the *Golden Shoe* I'd like to talk to,' Dawlish said. 'It looks as if I'll have to find more pressure to put on Orde, doesn't it? I think I can get it at the restaurant.'

'Why?'

He told her about Johnny and the manager of the other restaurant, and glanced at her when he finished. She nodded, as if she understood, and didn't comment on the fact that he hadn't told her before. The hatred, the lust for blood, had gone. He was surprised how easily he could talk to her; how easy it was to forget the way she had looked at those two men, and how ruthlessly she had killed one. He kept thinking about it. There was no doubt that the dead man had been trying to get a gun from his shoulder holster; little doubt that he would have killed. So she had saved his life. It would be easy to say that she needn't have killed the man, could have wounded him; but she hadn't had much time to make up her mind, and there hadn't been much margin of error. The man's arm had been across his chest, and to make him snatch it away she had to shoot his arm—or his head. If Dawlish looked at what he knew as evidence, he would have to acquit her of murder; she had shot to save her companion's life.

In his heart, he was afraid that she had shot to kill.

Whenever he glanced at her, she was relaxed, not smiling, but with a misty look in her eyes; she noticed whenever he glanced her way, and smiled.

'Thanks, Vanessa,' he said abruptly.

'For what, Pat?'

'As it had to be the driver or me, I'm glad it wasn't me.'

'I can't understand you,' she said slowly. 'I just can't understand that you've done what you have and been what you have, yet care about killing a rat like that. You must be good, or Orde wouldn't . . .' She paused for a moment, and then went on very swiftly, 'Orde wouldn't have sent that photograph to Klimm, would he?'

'I'm wondering who else has a photograph.'

'Here's something,' she said, and opened the dashboard pocket and took out a folded newspaper; it was only part of one, and was folded so that a photograph showed. He glanced down—at Vanessa's picture. She had her hair long, in this likeness, and wore an evening gown which the old-fashioned would have called daring; nothing could disguise the surpassing beauty. The odd thing was that she looked what the photograph suggested: bold—bad. Evil. And now she looked at him with those glowing eyes with laughter in them and laughter on her lips, as if she were too young to be evil, or even really bad.

'Where did you get this?'

'At the gas station,' she said. 'I asked if they had one for me to read.'

He could imagine her having the nerve to do that; and he could imagine that she knew if she took the newspaper away from the gas station, the man who had served her wouldn't have it to look at again.

'It's good in its way,' he said, 'but I'm not sure you're going to be recognized from it.'

'If they'd used one taken five years ago I would have been recognized,' Vanessa said, and actually laughed. 'I feel that much younger!'

He believed her.

As they sped back along the road, he kept glancing at and marvelling at her. She was so very gay—and yet she had killed without compunction and, worse, had been able to terrify a grown man, a killer in his own right, with a look.

Her hand rested on his leg lightly.

'What are you going to do when you reach the *Golden Shoe*?' she asked. It was when they were halfway back; and they hadn't been talking about that or anything else. She spoke as if it didn't really matter, and that she was asking for the sake of asking.

He grinned.

'I'm going to kidnap the manager,' he said. 'He's a friend of Orde, I fancy. I let Klimm go to give Orde that message. Now if I snatch one of his men, he'll get worried. I may be able to blackmail him into easing off the pressure.'

She said very slowly: 'I see. Listen, Pat. He's a friend of Orde you *guess* or you *imagine*—you could even *reckon*—if you still want to learn the language. When will you go? After dark?'

'As soon as we reach the *Golden Shoe*,' Dawlish told her.

CHAPTER XI

PRISONER

It was still broad daylight when they passed the *Golden Shoe.* The restaurant was much busier than when Johnny had gone into it. So were others, nearby. There was more private car traffic but few trucks. The evening was unpleasantly warm; men wore shirts which flapped against their bodies, most of the women were in flimsy cotton dresses.

Vanessa looked cool.

Vanessa had been so sweet, so demure, since they had left the *Silver Slipper,* that it was hard to believe she was the same woman. She didn't refer to the shooting; nothing suggested that it was in her mind at all. If she had trodden on an ant, she couldn't have been more indifferent. Yet indifferent wasn't quite the word; she behaved as if it really didn't matter, as if it did not occur to her to think about it.

'Don't you get hungry sometimes?' she asked. They had passed the *Golden Shoe,* and were still travelling fast.

'We're always eating,' Dawlish said. 'There's a restaurant we can stop at further along the road—out of sight of this place.' He slowed down. The second restaurant, which he had noticed that morning, had a dozen cars outside. 'It will be dark before we're ready, after all,' he said.

'How are you going to snatch him, Pat?'

'I don't know yet,' he said, and grinned.

The only time they parted was when they went to the rest-rooms. Vanessa was gone for nearly fifteen minutes. That meant that she had plenty of time to change. Dawlish sat smoking and waiting for her. He felt self-conscious, because his hair was now very dark; when he caught sight of his reflection, he gulped. It hadn't been easy; but the cold-water hair dye in a collapsible bowl by the side of a stream had been sufficient. If had taken over two hours.

He wished Vanessa would come.

When a waitress passed, he smiled as if she were the only woman in the world.

'What's good tonight?' He tried to use the intonation which Vanessa had been teaching him.

'Why, the Virginia ham's just wonderful,' the girl said, 'and the chicken in the basket couldn't be better, I guess.' She had the kind of sing-song voice which seemed unreal—and made him give up all hope of ever being able to talk 'American'. 'Or you could have a steak, sir, the steaks here are just wonderful.'

'Give me time to decide,' Dawlish said, and added as an after-thought: 'Is there a telephone in the ladies' rest-room?'

'Why, no, sir, the telephones are right there.' The girl pointed to the booth.

He nodded thanks, and went out for two minutes, walking right round the restaurant, making sure there was no other way Vanessa could get out, even if she wanted to. He wasn't sure what to make of Vanessa; he was only sure that he had to be extraordinarily watchful with her. He didn't yet know for sure why she had come with him in the first place, or why she stayed.

He hadn't been back two minutes when she came out. She

looked breathtakingly lovely. She made men stare. Yet she wasn't the Vanessa of the photograph, she was so much younger, simpler—little more than a girl.

'Wonderful,' he greeted her, getting up.

She smiled at him radiantly. . . .

'What's it to be?'

'I know it's crazy,' she said, 'but I feel just like chicken in the basket. You ever had chicken in the basket? You *haven't*?' Her voice rose, but it wasn't likely that anyone else heard. 'You just have to try it!'

He tried it. . . .

Hot, succulent chicken, eaten with the fingers, straight from a basket; salad; peaches; cream. He ate until he wanted nothing more. He ate until it would be easy to forget what he had come back here to do.

It was getting dark.

They went out.

The stars were just breaking the misty blue of the heavens with a brightness which seemed to be much nearer than a million miles away. Cars were putting their lights on. There seemed to be a hush upon the evening; there were no voices; there was the hum of insects and the hum of engines, and Vanessa's arm was linked in Dawlish's and pressed gently against him as they walked towards the car.

'Pat.'

'Yes?'

'I'm going to ask you again—do you have to go on with this? We could find a place where we could forget all about it. Just you and me.' She made the words seem like a caress.

'And every morning I'd wake up and wonder if this were the morning we were going to be captured or shot or got ready for the hangman,' Dawlish said.

'I'd make you forget, Pat.'

'Don't forget too much or too easily,' Dawlish said. 'Your husband was killed, and both you and I could be charged with his murder. I've other troubles, too. If Orde wants it that way, he could produce witnesses which would make sure that we didn't escape. I'm fond of life, Vanessa.'

'You can't live with this *all* the time.'

He grinned, shifted his arm, hugged her tightly and then kissed her full on the lips.

Dawlish walked slowly along the road towards the *Golden Shoe*. By night, the sign above it flashed on and off, a gleaming yellow which might have been taken for gold. No one on the highway could miss it—any more than they could miss the *Silver Slipper*, a hundred miles nearer the lumber camp, and the so-called fabulous redwoods.

The name itself was in foot-high letters which flashed on and off, now lighting up Dawlish's face and dark hair, now leaving him in shadows.

Twenty yards along the road, on the other side, Vanessa sat at the wheel of the Chevrolet.

He went into the restaurant.

Half the tables were full; half of the guests were in tuxedos. Three musicians in one corner made up a band which played dance music softly, with beautiful rhythm. No one took any notice of Dawlish. Two or three men and women were at the bar where he had had a drink when waiting to see what had happened to Johnny.

He didn't order a drink this time.

He went straight to the door where Johnny had come out and tapped. He waited. No one took any notice of him. A waiter in black dinner suit and black tie murmured an apology as he pushed past to get to the serving door.

This door opened, and a pretty girl with red hair looked up at him—ready to scowl, ready to show a poker face. After one long, lingering look, she smiled.

'Hi,' she said.

Dawlish grinned down at her. 'Hi. Is the manager in?'

'I guess he'll see you.' she said, and stood on one side. He entered a small room, which had a desk with a typewriter on it, some filing cabinets, several easy chairs, and a small table with a bowl of flowers on it. The room was cool, and the scent of the flowers pleasant. The girl didn't come up to Dawlish's shoulder. She was undoubtedly a pretty little thing, fresh and neat. 'What do you want to see him about?'

'I've a message,' Dawlish said. 'From Cy Klimm.'

'You're from *Cy*,' she said, as if that explained everything. 'Sure, I'll tell him.'

Dawlish's hand hardly appeared to move; but a twenty-dollar bill appeared between his thumb and forefinger.

'Alone,' he said.

Her eyes danced. 'Why, sure!' She took the bill and folded it, then thrust it inside the neck of her dress. She winked. 'Want to wait a minute?'

She opened the other door, and it swung behind her. Dawlish examined it carefully. It was very heavy, and closed without a sound; he thought that it was steel, and he wouldn't be surprised if he learned that it was electrically controlled, or could be electrically locked. There was one long window, with Venetian blinds which were down. On the table were several different advertising folders, about the Redwood Empire—and hotels, motor courts and restaurants on the highway were listed. There were several paper serviettes, with a simple map of the highway printed on them, and the names of certain hotels and motor courts, restaurants and night spots. The *Golden Shoe*—the

Silver Slipper—the *Long Stocking*—the *Shake a Leg*—there were a dozen or more. Dawlish folded several of the serviettes and slipped them in his pocket.

The girl came out.

'It's okay,' she said, and let the door close. She didn't smile again, but said quickly, softly, 'Don't stay too long, Mr. Benoni's busy.'

'Thanks, baby.' He pulled the door open. It swung easily, and yet he knew that it was heavy, was quite sure that it was of steel; and was probably bullet-proof. That mattered more than he had realized. He strode through a little hallway or recess, and then into another room, the door of which stood open. The manager, the man who had patted Johnny on the shoulder and assured him that there was no need to worry, was sitting at a big desk.

He looked affluent—white tuxedo, red bow tie, thin black hair glossed down, long and expensive-looking cigar sticking out of a pale face, like a miniature rocket bomb. He wasn't unlike Cyrus Klimm, except that his eyes didn't pop and he wasn't quite so flabby. There was the diamond solitaire ring on his right hand. He didn't make any attempt to get up, just looked at Dawlish—and as the door closed behind Dawlish it seemed as if the manager knew there was trouble.

He stiffened.

His right hand dropped below the level of the table; his fingers were probably at a bell-push.

Dawlish said amiably: 'Don't press it, don't send for anyone else. If you do, I'll kill you.'

Benoni didn't move, didn't show any expression, but after a moment he brought his hand into sight. He rested it on the top of the desk. There was no way of telling whether he had pressed an alarm bell or not. Dawlish backed a little towards a corner, from which he was in no danger from windows or the doors. He smiled all the time.

'We're going places,' he said. 'Get up.'

'You don't know—'

'You won't get hurt,' Dawlish said. 'That is, you won't get hurt much so long as you do what you're told. Just think what happened to Johnny and remember that two can play the same game.'

Benoni began to speak, quickly and in a low-pitched voice. There was a sense of urgency in his manner, but that was all— no outward sign of fear, flurry or excitement.

'Listen, Dawlish, you're asking for trouble. You and me can go places together if you'll talk sense. Now sit down, have a drink, forget—'

'Get up, Benoni.' Dawlish said. 'I'm not going to waste time or chances. Either you come with me or you stay here—and if you stay here you'll be a corpse. One more or less won't make any difference.' His smile was slow; he looked huge and almost indifferent as he took a gun out of his pocket. He didn't glance down at it, but pointed it at Benoni's face.

No one appeared at the windows; no one opened the door.

Benoni stood up.

'Where are we going?'

'I'll tell you just as soon as I've made Orde see reason,' Dawlish said. 'Go to the restaurant door, stand there facing it until I tell you to move. Then you'll lead the way, and we'll go out. I shall blow a hole in your back if you shout or raise an alarm at all. Understand?'

Benoni swallowed.

'Sure,' he said. 'Sure, I understand.' Dawlish thought that he did; believed that he knew he was near death. Much—everything—would depend on his believing that. There was no way of being sure that he hadn't pressed an alarm bell; that no one would be waiting at this door or at the main restaurant door.

Benoni went to the door, as instructed. He was shorter than Dawlish remembered, stocky, but not fat. He had rather slanting eyes, and flashed a look at Dawlish from the corners as he passed. He stood still, with his back to Dawlish, Dawlish went closer to him.

'Benoni,' he said, 'my right hand's in my pocket with the fore-finger on the trigger. If you don't do what I say, I shall shoot you. Open the door and walk towards the restaurant. Say something to your secretary—say you won't be long. Then cross the restau-rant and go outside. I'll talk to you again outside.' Benoni didn't answer. He pushed the door, and it opened. Dawlish watched tensely, looking over his head, expecting to see a legman, fully expecting trouble.

Only the girl was there.

'I'll be back, Peggy,' Benoni said with a glance at the girl, and went towards the restaurant door.

CHAPTER XII

THE *GOLDEN SHOE*

Dawlish didn't glance behind him, but felt sure that the girl didn't get up, didn't see anything unusual in this. He held his breath as Benoni opened the door leading to the restaurant. A waiter was coming, and glanced his way. For a split second Dawlish thought that trouble was on him; then the waiter passed.

Benoni went straight to the outer door, without looking right or left. He didn't fuss, didn't do anything to suggest that he was frightened, or that he was trying to give anyone else a warning. He almost swaggered. Dawlish watched that other door, for there was still time for the counter-attack.

Benoni opened the door.

They stepped out beneath the flashing, glittering light of the *Golden Shoe*. A car drew up, and people laughed and shouted as they spilled out. A motor-cycle cop passed, travelling slowly. Two or three people stood about by gas stations and motor courts, but no one appeared to take any notice of Dawlish and Benoni.

The Chevrolet was drawn up, close by—Vanessa was at the wheel. He had told her to give him ten minutes; he had probably taken three or four more. She leaned out and opened the door. She looked at Benoni as she did so—and Benoni missed a step. He wasn't a craven; he might believe that he was walking to his death, but until the moment that he set eyes on Vanessa he didn't show any sign of it. Now, he missed that step. Dawlish couldn't see his face, but he saw Vanessa's. He could imagine that she had looked like this when she had wanted to kill the two men on the beach; and when she had killed the man in the red shirt. It was hard to say what happened to her face, the features were relaxed, her eyes were wide open, and yet the expression hardened, did more than harden.

She looked as if she hated.

She turned away, and Dawlish put a hand on Benoni's shoulder and guided him to the back of the car. By the time he got in next to the restaurant manager, Vanessa was at the wheel. She drove off. In a few minutes they were out of sight of the *Golden Shoe.*

Vanessa slowed down.

'So you did it,' she said, and looked round at Dawlish, smiling. 'That's wonderful!'

'I'm going to do more,' Dawlish said. 'I'm going back to search his office. Give me your keys, Benoni.'

Benoni said, 'Daw—'

'Give me your keys,' Dawlish repeated, and struck the man beneath the jaw. It wasn't a hard punch; it wasn't anything like the savage blow which Benoni would have given if the situation were reversed.

Benoni took out his keys and handed them over.

'Wallet,' Dawlish said briefly.

Benoni handed that over, too. Even in the light from the motels and restaurant which they passed, his nails showed— filbert-shaped and shiny with polish.

'Draw off the road, Vanessa,' Dawlish said. They had turned and almost reached the *Golden Shoe* again, could pick out the shape of the flashing advertisement. 'And wait for me.'

She didn't answer.

'Dawlish—' began Benoni, and hesitated.

'What?'

'Don't—leave me alone with her.'

Dawlish said, 'Unless you try to get away, you'll be all right.' He got out of the car as Vanessa switched off the engine. She looked round, picking up her handbag as she did so; and she opened it and took out the gun. 'I want to talk to him again, Vanessa,' Dawlish went on mildly, 'don't make any mistake this time.'

'All right,' she said. 'But he'd better sit still.'

'Vanessa,' said Dawlish, very softly, 'I do not want him dead. Understand?'

They eyed each other. . . .

She looked away first. Dawlish smiled faintly, turned, and walked towards the *Golden Shoe*.

The girl Peggy was sitting at her desk, smoking. She looked up when Dawlish entered, and smiled again without considering him this time.

'Why, hallo,' she said, and glanced behind him, as if for Benoni. 'Where's the boss?'

'He won't be long,' Dawlish said. 'I have to wait for him, beautiful.' He winked at her as he pushed open the door of the inner office. She didn't argue or protest. He let the door close, and looked for a keyhole; there wasn't one. So it was electrically controlled—and if anyone became suspicious, they could seal him in.

He hadn't much time.

He spared a closer look at the windows. He soon found that these were of toughened glass, and would be difficult to break. Worse—he saw the metal which ran through the panes. In emergency, electric current could be passed through them, and would probably be strong enough to kill.

It made him very thoughtful; and it made him in a greater hurry. He used Benoni's keys to open two locked drawers in the desk, and found little there. Some papers, account books, records, and a diary. He slipped the diary into his pocket, and looked through all the other papers again, sure that he could remember them, and would know if they took on any significance later. Then he went to the safe, in a corner. It was covered by a wooden shell; until he opened the polished pine door he couldn't be sure that it was the safe.

He opened it.

He found jewel cases; stacks of dollar bills—mostly hundreds—and some letters and his own photograph. On the back were scrawled the words: *Dawlish—I told you about him on the telephone.* Dawlish scanned the letters; they seemed to be innocuous enough, and about legal business. There were several addresses in a loose-leaf book, and one address cropped up several times:

Ole Ben Lumber Camp, Riall County, Calif.

There wasn't much doubt—that was Orde's place. So this was a stage nearer; and with so much achieved there was reason for hope.

Dawlish wished that he could find more about himself, about Vanessa, Haffmeyer and Kell—about anything. Nothing else here really helped him. For the second time he turned to leave this room, wondering what would happen when he got outside—then wondering if he would be able to open the door.

He pulled at it.

It wouldn't open.

He stood quite still by the door, with a hand close to the handle but no longer on it. His fingers seemed to tingle—as they would if a slight electric shock had run through him. He looked at the handle and the blank surface of the door, which had no keyhole. He had heard no sound, had no reason to think that anyone had cause for suspicion.

He tried again.

The door wouldn't open.

He turned away from it, slowly, and went towards the desk. He leaned against it, took out cigarettes and lit one very slowly. He watched the flame die down as he held the match between his finger and thumb. He could hear no sound. He did not know who was at the door—did not know for certain whether he could be seen.

The silence was the worst part of it—the silence and the knowledge that he couldn't get out. When he said those words to himself, they seemed to have a curious kind of finality. He felt less frightened than fatalistic; as if he had known all the time that the odds were too great, and that he hadn't really a chance.

He drew at the cigarette.

He felt that he was being watched, and looked slowly about the room. There were a dozen places in the wall and the ceiling which might conceal a spy-hole. It was very cool, everything was luxurious—and there was that deathly silence.

A bell jarred through it.

Dawlish started violently, the noise came so sharply, so

unexpectedly. It was the telephone. He looked at it as it rang again. It was over on a corner of the desk, near where Benoni's left hand should have been. He moved towards it as it rang for a third time.

He lifted it. 'Hallo.'

'*Are* you Dawlish?' a girl asked.

He was quite sure that it was Benoni's secretary. He wasn't quite sure whether the questions was anything more than rhetorical.

'*Are* you?' repeated the girl.

'I don't get it,' said Dawlish. 'I came to see Benoni and he's taken a powder.' He uttered every word carefully, praying that he had the right inflection, that he wouldn't sound English. There was no immediate answer. He imagined that the girl was sitting at her desk—but he couldn't be sure who else was with her. 'I haven't got all night; when is he coming back?'

'Don't you *know*?'

'What *is* this? demanded Dawlish peevishly. 'Benoni told me he would be right back.'

'I—see,' said the girl. He thought she sounded nervous.

'Listen,' Dawlish said, 'I'll come and talk to you.'

He put down the receiver, and looked at the door. He had tried to make her believe that he didn't known that the door was locked. If she really believed that, she might unlock it so that he could go into her office. The office would be watched, but he was sure that if he could get out of this room, he would have a chance.

Vanessa wasn't far away, with Benoni.

If the people here were suspicious of him now, they might have been suspicious before, might have followed him; might now be watching Vanessa.

He reached the door and turned the handle—there was no

trouble. His heart began to thump. He pulled open the door and stepped into the smaller office. Peggy wasn't alone. Two men were with her, one of them sitting on her desk, the other standing by the door. They were sleek and well dressed—and Dawlish was quite sure that they were Orde's men, legmen; that they were armed and would kill if they thought it necessary—and safe. The one on the desk looked older and more deadly. He had his right hand in his pocket.

'Where's Benoni?' he asked.

Dawlish heard the door close behind him softly. He looked at the man impatiently. He prayed that he looked as if he were annoyed, as if he couldn't understand the question.

'Why ask me?'

'He went out with you, pal. He didn't come back with you.'

Dawlish decided not to stall.

'He sent me ahead,' he said.

'That's what we don't believe,' the man said. He sent a sideways glance towards the man at the door, as if warning him to be very careful now. 'Where did you take him?'

Dawlish said, 'You're crazy.' He looked at Peggy; he hoped it was a resigned, puzzled look, a 'do-you-know-what-he's-talking-about?' look. He put a hand to his pocket and saw the men stiffen, expecting him to go for a gun. He took out cigarettes, shook one from the packet, then lit it. He put the cigarettes back and flicked the match towards an ash-tray.

It landed.

'I told Benoni I was in a hurry,' he said. 'Klimm wanted—'

'Why did Klimm send a guy we didn't know?' asked the man sitting on the corner of the desk. It was obvious that the question really worried him; as obvious that if he could get the right answer, he would be satisfied. Dawlish went a little nearer the desk, but not nearer the man. The other, by the door, shifted his position so that he could keep Dawlish in sight all the time.

'Why don't you ask Klimm? There's the telephone.'

'He's not at the *Slipper*,' the man said, and looked worried.

'He's not been in all day, he's gone to—'

'Old Ben?'

The man licked his lips, as if that statement surprised him, and he knew that he ought to do something but wasn't quite sure what it ought to be.

'Could be. How do you know—?'

Dawlish couldn't stand still any longer. He was quite sure that he couldn't bluff them into letting him go; they would hold him until they were sure of him—and there was no way in which they could become sure. So he had to fight.

He moved sideways, both hands shooting out. He grabbed the man on the desk by his right arm. In a split second a gun roared—the gun in the man's pocket. He heard the man gasp. He saw Peggy jump up from her chair as he sent the man hurtling across the room towards the guard at the door. It was the one moment that mattered—forcing the guard to move, making sure that he couldn't take proper aim.

He heard the second shot, and wondered if they could hear it in the restaurant, but didn't give himself much time for wondering. He flung himself forward, and a bullet went over his head. His hands clutched the gunman's feet. He knew that if the man trained the gun down, a head of newly dyed hair could be split in two. He clenched his teeth, waiting for the bullet.

It was an agonizing second of uncertainty—and in it the guard lost his balance as Dawlish tugged, and crashed down.

Dawlish got to his feet, turned his back on the door, drew his gun out.

'Hold it.' he said.

He could deal with these three now; he couldn't deal with anyone in the restaurant, *if* they had heard.

Was this room soundproof, too?

CHAPTER XIII

NIGHT

The man who had been sitting on the desk was leaning against it heavily. There was blood on his coat and trousers; he had shot himself accidentally. His hands were in sight, the gun wasn't; the pain of the shooting must have made him snatch his hand away.

Peggy was in a strange position; half standing, half sitting. She looked petrified, as if she couldn't move up or down; as if, like Lot's wife, she had been turned into a pillar. She was pretty, but for the way her mouth twisted; she was terrified, too.

All of these people frightened easily; were on edge.

The man by the door was on the floor now, and his gun was a couple of yards from his hand. There was no immediate danger from the trio; it was as if a tornado had hit them.

There might be danger from the restaurant, remember.

Dawlish could try to make Peggy talk or he could take a chance.

He said: 'Benoni's outside with a friend of mine. If I'm not back in a few minutes, Benoni will be as dead as—'

He didn't finish.

He put his hand to his pocket, hiding the gun, opened the

door with his other hand. He had to watch the trio and see what was happening in the restaurant. No one was outside the door, no one was ready for trouble. A waiter scurried by, heavily laden.

'And Benoni wouldn't like that,' Dawlish said.

He pulled the door wide, and stepped out. The door closed slowly. He saw one man move, but Peggy stayed as she was until the door cut her off from his sight. Dawlish swallowed hard as he turned towards the outer door. No one took any notice of him. There was a clatter in the restaurant, a hum of conversation, a man laughing and the orchestra playing; but he had heard nothing from Peggy's office, which suggested that that was soundproof, too.

He reached the door.

No one came out of the office.

He went out, and the night air was warm compared with the air-conditioned rooms. He gulped in air and he strode towards the Chevrolet, which was two hundred yards along—or should be. He looked over his shoulder, but no one came out of the restaurant.

He found it hard to believe that they would let him get away with it so easily.

He saw the Chevrolet, moving towards him. Vanessa had eyes which could compete with a hawk's.

He forced himself to walk; not to break into a run.

He saw one man, then another, come from the back of the *Golden Shoe,* and run towards a car. If they had walked he would have thought nothing of it—their running was the danger signal. By the time they were in the car, the Chevrolet was almost level with him.

He snatched at the door as it slowed down. It didn't actually stop. Benoni should have been in his way, at the back—but he couldn't see Benoni. He thought of the men running from the restaurant; of the fact that they would soon be driving towards him, would know that they were after a powder-blue Chevrolet. He thought of Benoni, who wasn't here, who ought to be, who—

Benoni was a crumpled heap on the floor.

Dawlish dropped into the seat. Vanessa stepped on the accelerator and the car shot forward. The men who had come from the *Golden Shoe* were moving towards the road; they wouldn't be more than thirty seconds behind.

Dawlish and Vanessa flashed by.

Other cars were coming behind them, but the car with Benoni's men in it ignored them and swung into the stream of traffic, forcing cars to swerve, to brake, sending one skidding to the other side of the road. The driver had gained ten seconds; Dawlish had only twenty seconds' lead. The other car was a Cadillac, with more power and more speed.

There was one thing to do, and only one.

Dawlish leaned out of the window, gun in hand.

He fired four times; on the fourth, the pursuing car swerved violently across the road, hit a tree, and seemed to stand on its nose.

All this time, Vanessa drove as if she were having a pleasant evening's outing.

Here, it was very dark.

There were the stars; but there were no other lights near them. The *Golden Shoe* and Highway 99 were ten miles to the east. Not far ahead was Highway 101 and the Pacific—but it was too far away for them to reach tonight. They had travelled along a country road, then on a dirt track which led over farmland for a while, then towards trees. Now, they were among the trees, friendly and sheltered.

Vanessa stopped the car, and switched off the parking lights. She didn't appear to turn her head, but he heard the rustle of her movements. A match flared. She turned, this time, and he saw the glowing tip held out towards him. He didn't take the cigarette.

'I thought I told you I wanted to talk to Benoni,' he said.

'What's to stop you?' Vanessa asked.

'He's—'

'Pat for Patrick,' Vanessa said, 'for a man who's done the things you're supposed to have done, you're very softhearted. He would have caused trouble. I just slugged him.' It was too dark to see her face; but he could imagine the gleam of her teeth as she smiled. 'He'll be okay.'

Dawlish knew that Benoni was alive, because he had felt the man's pulse. He hadn't known whether she had shot him or not; he knew now. Her voice was calm, she wasn't flustered, and she wasn't really frightened. That made him think of the time they had met, when she had come silently upon him with the gun. She hadn't been frightened then, although afterwards she had seemed to be.

'But he'd be safer dead,' she said.

'I never liked corpses.' Dawlish took the cigarette, which was still held out to him. 'Thanks. We can't use this car any longer.'

He was more amazed than ever that they hadn't been stopped by the police. He felt more sure than ever that the police could have picked them up—if they wanted to. But the police seemed determined to let him and Orde fight this out. Instructions would come from people in high places.

But when the police wanted to pounce, they would.

'We've plenty of money,' she said. 'We can buy a new car. We're taking so many chances we can take some more.' There was almost laughter in her voice.

'We'll wait a while before we buy,' Dawlish said. He drew hard at the cigarette, and tried to decide what to do.

They were five hundred miles from Riall County and the lumber mill—and Orde. No one at the *Golden Shoe* would want to talk much about what had happened, but when the police started questioning, much of the truth would come out. They would expect to find Benoni, and would ask where he was—and guess that he was missing. But there was one thing that might explain the fact that they hadn't searched and found Dawlish. The police might reasonably expect the driver of the powder-blue Chevrolet to get as far away as he could. They wouldn't expect him to be on their doorsteps.

He had to get another different car.

There was Benoni, still unconscious; when she had slugged him, Vanessa hadn't shown much mercy. Benoni might know a great deal, and had to be questioned soon. In any case, they couldn't leave him here.

Could they?

What were the chances of the car being found here, in the woods? In the darkness, negligible. In the morning—there wasn't even a way of knowing whether it could be seen or whether the bush would hide it from anyone passing on the nearby road.

Vanessa sat smoking.

Dawlish looked through the diary. Now and again there were entries reading: '*Meet O. at Camp*', or '*O. called.*' Apparently Orde and Benoni met most weeks.

There was nothing else to help.

"What's in your mind?' Vanessa asked.

Dawlish said, 'Listen, Vanessa—'

The suitcase was heavy, but it was the one thing they had had to carry. It contained the money and Vanessa's oddments of clothes. The clothes didn't weigh much, but the money seemed to weigh a ton.

They had walked for an hour, first through the trees, then along a road which was hardly a road, more like a track which might lead further into the woods; only it didn't. There were no trees now, just open land, visible in the stars.

Benoni was tied hand and foot, back in the Chevrolet. He had come round—and Dawlish had examined his wound, and convinced himself that Benoni wasn't as badly hurt as he pretended. He hadn't spent time questioning the man then—He had a hostage, and meant to keep him; and he had made sure that Orde had agents stationed along the highway.

What they needed was a place where they could safely leave Benoni, knowing that he wouldn't be found either by the police or by Orde's men.

Suddenly, Vanessa caught his arm.

She had walked well, said little, seemed prepared to go on all night. Now she grew tense. He saw her arm, as she pointed; and a moment later picked out the shape of a house against the sky.

They drew nearer.

There were lights at the house, visible from the other side. Outbuildings, too—and a garage. Music sounded—and if there were music inside the room, then whoever was there would have less chance of hearing sounds outside.

They found the double garage. The doors were open, and a jeep stood next to an old black car. A key was needed—and Dawlish made do with a piece of wire, after they had pushed the ancient car out of the garage and towards the dirt road. Soon they were travelling back towards the woods—and Benoni.

With Benoni in the back of the stolen car, a Pontiac which had seen much better days, they headed south again.

*   *   *

It was broad daylight when Dawlish woke. He felt stiff, dry and headachy. At first he hardly realized where he was. Then he remembered that they had pulled off the road and hidden themselves in a valley not far from Highway 99—and gone to sleep. Well, he had slept. He didn't know for certain about Vanessa. She wasn't in the car, although she had been the night before.

He looked round. Benoni was there, sleeping, with his mouth slightly open; he made little popping noises. He did not look attractive, anyway, and he needed a shave badly. Dawlish ran his hand over his own stubble, and realized that he himself needed one even more. He would have to get one, or would be noticeable because of his fair beard.

He got out of the car, awkwardly.

There wasn't a cloud in the sky. There was the hum of traffic some way off; now and again a high-pitched whine made him think that the road was actually nearer than it was. He wanted to see Vanessa, but couldn't.

The country was soft and enchanting—in the distance there were orchards, nearby were groves of maple. There was broken country, with thick, coarse grass and clumps of dogwood, its bloom almost gone.

But no Vanessa.

He wished it weren't so hot.

He wished he were not so worried about Vanessa.

He made sure that Benoni's bonds were tight enough, then moved away. He needed a drink badly, and he wanted to smoke; he wouldn't enjoy a smoke until he had moistened his parched mouth. Everything was going wrong, although Orde was only three hundred and fifty miles away, for they had travelled fast during the early hours. But in some ways the man was as far as a million miles off.

Dawlish reached the top of the hill.

A valley fell away from here, grass- and tree-clad on both soft sides, a soft and gentle scene. Far off, he could see the blue of the ocean; much nearer, the silvery blue of a stream, and in the stream, Vanessa, naked as the day she was born, lying and looking towards him.

CHAPTER XIV

THE TALL TREES

She did not move.

The crystal-clear water ran over her body. Her head was raised, slightly, resting on a boulder. The water eddied and swirled gently, and sang. It washed the stones in the river bed clean—so clean that some of them looked as soft and blemishless as Vanessa's body. She smiled faintly, but made no great effort; if she called him, it was with her eyes.

He stood a few yards off, looking at her.

'Cool in there, Vanessa?'

'It's just wonderful.'

'How long have you been here?'

'Oh, half an hour or more, I guess.'

'Why didn't you wake me?'

'It seemed a shame, you were so tired,' she said, 'and I didn't think you would want to intrude on my privacy.' Her smile was still faint, lazy. 'Why don't you have a bathe, Pat? And you can have a drink, too—just upstream.' She raised her right arm and pointed languidly.

He turned away.

Not far off, the water dropped over several boulders, making a tiny waterfall, as clear and limpid as water could ever be, and catching the sun. He stooped down, made a cup of his hands, and drank. It was everything she had promised and everything he desired. He took off his coat and shirt, stretched, and then knelt by the stream and washed his face, his back and chest. The temptation to do what she was doing was great—almost too great. The temptation she offered in every way was nearly overwhelming; but it would be good for him and better for her if he resisted it—while he could.

Finished, he strolled towards her, taking out his cigarettes and lighting one. He didn't offer it to her. Her face was above water, but her hair was soaking. She hadn't moved. She was surpassingly beautiful, and she looked so young, a nymphlike creature—oh, she had the qualities to put all the old hackneyed phrases into his head. She looked like the running water—*pure.* She spread her fingers and let the water disport itself between and among them—and he remembered that they were the fingers which had held a gun; that forefinger had squeezed, to kill a man.

The sun dried him.

'Hungry?' he asked.

'Pat called Patrick,' she said, 'I'm beginning to believe some of the things I was told about Englishmen.'

'Such as?'

'How cold-blooded they are!'

He grinned, finished his cigarette, dropped it and trod it out, and then stood up. Vanessa's clothes were in a little pile not far from the bank; with them was a towel. He rubbed his own hair briskly. His eyes were covered with the towel, and saw nothing; and because he was rubbing vigorously, he heard nothing. When he stopped and took the towel away, she was in front of him, water dripping from her body—and from her hair, which hung like rats' tails about her neck.

'I just hate drying my own hair,' she said.

'We can't have that,' said Dawlish. He dropped the towel over her head and rubbed vigorously. She knew exactly what she was doing. She didn't move at all, added nothing to the moment. He didn't wait to judge whether her hair was dry enough, just gave it a final brisk rub, and let the towel fall over her shoulders. 'Don't hurry,' she said, 'it's too hot for hurrying.'

He walked off.

They had breakfast at a little place not far away—bacon and eggs, wheatcakes and maple syrup and coffee; it was almost a staple diet. They took sandwiches and some milk to Benoni, who, while they were eating, was on the floor at the back of the car, with a rug over him. They lingered for half an hour, while Dawlish shaved in the restaurant's rest-room. Then Dawlish tackled Benoni.

The man was scared, but he kept his nerve. Vanessa worried him at least as much as Dawlish—if not more. He answered most questions, but not freely.

'Of course I know Mr Orde, Dawlish. He's an old friend of mine.'

'Why did he kill Haffmeyer?'

'That's a funny idea, Dawlish; he wouldn't kill anyone.'

'Why did he give orders to kill me?'

'I've had no such orders, Dawlish.'

'Klimm had.'

'If Klimm said that, he lied,' Benoni said.

'What's Orde's racket?' Vanessa asked sharply. 'What does he do?'

'He's just a business man,' Benoni claimed. 'That's all.'

Dawlish could have broken him down; Vanessa wanted to. But there was time yet, and Dawlish was anxious to find out how Orde would react to the news of Benoni's capture. If he were too tough, it might lose him all chance of coming to terms with Orde; or pretending to.

'We'll talk to you again,' he said.

Under her breath, Vanessa said that he must be crazy.

They started out in the Pontiac.

At four o'clock in the afternoon they came upon the big trees.

Above everything, Dawlish had to see Orde and talk to him. It had become more than an obsession; it had become the only purpose in life, almost the reason for life—as it might prove to be. He had not been able to think beyond that for weeks; and for days past everything he had thought of had been guided by that final objective—to find Orde, to see him.

Now he was among the tall trees where Orde lived.

He had been dozing while Vanessa drove. It had been her suggestion some way back. They had stopped, Dawlish had eased Benoni's bonds, questioned the man again with the same result, given him a drink. Then he had sat by Vanessa's side, while the warm air swept in, and gradually the heat had made him drowsy; and he had dozed. He wasn't sure now what had woken him up— although there was a sensation, as if he had been touched sharply.

He looked up.

The day had darkened. There was no brightness, no hurtful, glaring sun; no vivid sky except that broken by a strange tracery of high branches. These were so high, the trees so tall, that they drove everything else out of his mind. They were unbelievable. It was as if he were going through a giant forest while he himself had shrunk to pigmy size. There were other cars ahead and behind, but they seemed tiny too; and everywhere there was a hush, as of evening.

Vanessa pulled off the road beneath some trees, where the ground was clear and a little grass grew.

'Well, did you know what to expect, Pat*rick*?' asked Vanessa, her eyes smiling.

He said, 'I don't believe it.'

'These aren't the really big ones.' Her eyes danced.

'I don't believe that either.'

'You'll find out,' she said: 'about the biggest redwoods are in Riall County.' Where Orde was, 'Orde's among the very biggest, I think. Aren't these *won*derful?'

'Wonderful is just a word,' Dawlish said. 'These are beyond words.' He hesitated. 'How high—' he began, and then stopped. 'No, I don't want to know.'

'Three hundred feet isn't really tall here.'

'Nonsense.'

'Three hundred and fifty is common and you can drive through some of them; holes have been cut in the trunks.'

'Imagination!'

'The tallest must be nearly four hundred feet and that would make them the tallest in the world.'

He looked at her with his head on one side and then got out. She got out the other side. He looked in at Benoni and then pulled the rug over the prisoner's face; no one could glance in casually and see the man. He joined Vanessa at the front of the car. She took his hand. Quite lightly, almost boy-with-girl, they walked hand in hand among the trees, looking upwards. Unless Dawlish held his head right back he could not see the tops of the near trees. The girths were fantastic. There was one huge one, not far off, and they went towards it and solemnly walked round it, Vanessa counting as they went.

'Forty-five feet,' she said.

'We're dreaming.'

'Pat.'

'Yes?'

'Orde isn't far away.' Vanessa said softly. 'Just a few miles now. Orde's very powerful. He uses killers. You won't have a chance with Orde. You just won't have a chance. Why don't you give it up? Why don't you come with me?'

He released her hand, faced her, put his hands on her shoulders and then kissed her. At first his lips pressed gently; gradually he increased the pressure until he could feel the hardness of her teeth; and as he kissed her he held her closer, crushing her body against his. Cars and trucks passed and a hundred people might have seen them, but he took no notice of glancing eyes.

He released her; she was short of breath.

'After I've finished with Orde,' he said, 'I'll have time for you.'

Vanessa said: 'They're all killers—from the top to the bottom they're killers. They have to be rubbed out, or they rub you out. You don't have to take chances, Pat. It's not worth it. There's you and me and a new world waiting for us.'

He grinned at her.

'As if I didn't know!' His eyes danced—and they could dance; he could be lighthearted and light of spirit, in spite of all that he knew about her and what he was about to face. 'After I've seen Orde we can think about ourselves.'

'If Orde hurts you.' she said very slowly, almost as if the words caused her pain, 'I shall kill him. Did you know how I felt about you?'

She wasn't smiling now.

'I guessed,' said Dawlish. He slid an arm round her waist and they moved back towards the car. 'Wait for a while, Vanessa, and leave the killing to me.'

She didn't answer.

'At the first telephone I'm going to call Orde again,' Dawlish said. 'But I don't think there's going to be any trouble seeing him now.'

'Why not?'

'The police might have been convinced that we'd gone a long way out of the district, but Orde knew we hadn't. Orde knows the day and the time when we were at the *Golden Shoe*. He would have the road watched. I wouldn't mind betting that he knows where we are to within a few miles. If he'd wanted to kill, we'd be dead by now.'

She said slowly; 'You may be right. What do you think has made him change his mind?'

'Benoni.'

'He could be fooling you,' Vanessa said. They were back by the car. 'You want to drive?'

'I think I will,' said Dawlish. 'I'm going to find somewhere to hide Benoni. Haven't I read about some caves near here?'

'They're way north, in Oregon.'

'We'll find somewhere else.'

Soon they turned off the road, among the giant trees. No one was with them, in front or behind. The road was narrow, stony and rutted; the car lurched, springs groaned. After nearly half an hour they reached a wooden bridge over a narrow river, with huge boulders on either side, and steep banks. Dawlish walked to the water's edge and studied the banks—then pointed.

There were caves.

'How did you know that?' Vanessa demanded.

'I read about them,' Dawlish said casually. 'This is where we'll leave Benoni.'

* * *

Back on the highway Dawlish drove slowly. He was thinking with half his mind that Orde was within a few miles—certainly within an hour's journey; and he was also thinking, with the rest of his mind, that the Redwood Empire was just that. The trees, huge beyond all dreams, hemmed them in.

He began to remember what he had read about them. Trees 3,000 years old—a thousand years before Christ these trees had been here, these very trees, already taller than He, perhaps already a hundred heet high. Here primitive man had lived and hunted, fished and killed. . . .

A car passed swiftly. There were two men in the front. One of them looked at them, and the car slowed down. Dawlish's thoughts were wrenched from the trees. The car went on more slowly, as if anxious that Dawlish should overtake it again. He didn't and it drew away.

Had he reason to be nervous of it?

They passed out of the great trees into a stretch of land where the trees were ordinary size; where there were orchards and cultivated fields. But soon they were among the fabulous trees again and then they came upon a restaurant where there would be a telephone.

He looked at the cars parked outside and recognized none of them. Vanessa went in for some coffee. He went straight to the telephone. He felt as if everyone were looking at him. His heart was beating fast again—threatening to suffocate him. He had only to put in ten cents and dial Orde's number, direct—not a long-distance call. Orde himself was within a few miles. He had to keep reminding himself of that.

He heard the ringing sound.

He waited. It seemed an age—so long, that he began to wonder whether there would be an answer. He felt his muscles go tense. He stared at Vanessa, and was conscious of everyone who stared at her, as if seeing past the fluffy auburn hair and the girl's face to the sophisticated woman of the newspaper photograph.

A familiar heavily accented voice said, 'Who iss dat?'

'Dawlish,' Dawlish said. 'Tell Orde I want to speak to him.'

He heard the man gasp; he could imagine what the man felt. He waited. His heart hammered again. A waitress was smiling at Vanessa, but two men at another table were staring at her fixedly—was that just because of her siren beauty, the fact that men couldn't keep their eyes away?

'Where—where *are* you?'

'Listen, I'm in a hurry,' Dawlish said. 'Let me speak to Orde. Tell him that if he doesn't, he won't see Benoni again.'

'All right, Dawlish,' Orde broke in. 'What is it you want?'

'That's better,' Dawlish said.

Dawlish left the telephone booth. He didn't smile, although his heart had stopped hammering, and some of the excitement had gone; as if life had reached a climax and he was now coasting downhill. Vanessa was sitting alone. The men nearby transferred their gaze to him; so did she. Her eyes were magnificent—seeming more golden-coloured than tawny, and she was obviously desperately anxious to know what he had to say.

He pushed his way into the seat opposite her.

'It's all arranged,' he said. 'I'm meeting him at the *Shoestring*, ten miles south of here, in two hours' time. You'll be with me, but we won't be together. You can take it from me, he's worried about Benoni.'

CHAPTER XV

THE *SHOESTRING*

Two hours and ten minutes from that moment gave them plenty of time. Dawlish wondered how best to use it. There were dozens of questions in his mind and he didn't need Vanessa's help with them. As he drove off she watched him closely. Now and again he saw that she was leaning back with her eyes narrowed, looking sideways at him. Her lips were parted and her teeth glistened.

He wanted more than ever to know what was in her mind, but one thing seemed certain. There was a change in her attitude towards him. It had been impersonal, but now she behaved as if he mattered to her, there was a possessive air about her. But that didn't explain Vanessa and her motives.

Why had she stayed so close to him?

He turned off the main road where a sign said TO THE BIG TREES. In a few minutes they were in the darkness of what might have been primeval forest. Sunlight shone a long way above their heads; only here and there was a shaft bright enough to reach the ground and to spread a faint glow. Looking up, Dawlish could see the mighty trunks and the tufts of branches at the top, so far away that they seemed small.

There were plenty of parking places.

He pulled into one of these. Now that he was more used to the light he saw other cars, gleaming dully; and people walking about, their heads craned to try to see to the tops of the trees. A well-worn path some way off was marked by a second sign and a huge hand pointing: *To The Big Trees.*

'You want to see the Big Trees?' Vanessa asked, and there was a hint of brittle laughter in her voice.

'We've time,' Dawlish said, and leaned across her and opened the door. She caught his arm and wouldn't let him withdraw it. She held it tightly against her, and still looked at him out of the corners of her eyes.

'You want to use the little time left to you the best way you can,' she said. She leaned towards him. Her lips were very close. He felt the touch of her breath. Then she kissed him.

She let him go.

He got out of the car and they met at the front. She slid her arm through his and walked away from the path and the big sign. Dawlish didn't speak. They could hear sounds. A long way off, it seemed, the cars on the highway hummed like fabulous insects. Nearer, there were crackling sounds, as if the twigs beneath their feet were splintering in a thousand places at the same time. Now and again there came the hushed voice of a man or woman; a kind of whispering. The whispering grew louder, and became the murmur of a wide stream which they reached after five minutes.

Here it was brighter; here the trees did not meet together at the top and the sunlight shone and their eyes were narrowed against it. The light shimmered and glimmered on the dancing water, there were great rocks and a gentle beauty everywhere, with the guardian trees keeping away all evil things.

'Pat,' Vanessa said.

'Yes?'

'You aren't going without some guarantees, are you?'

'Why not?'

'You can't be that crazy,' she said. 'He'll kill you. He's shown all the time that he wants to kill you; there's nothing he would rather do. Don't fool yourself that he's worried about Benoni.'

Dawlish sat down on a boulder and took out cigarettes.

'He hasn't made another attack,' he said. 'He's curious by now. I think I can hold his interest for a while.'

Vanessa said slowly; 'Pat, you can tell me the truth. *Are* you going to do a deal with Orde? Was Gurth right when he put a finger on you? Have you got secrets for sale?'

Dawlish offered her a cigarette and she took one. He lit hers, then his own. She moved slowly, deliberately, took the cigarette from his lips and tossed it into the river; then she tossed her own. Next she sat down beside him, so that she could face him.

'You haven't enough time left to smoke,' she said. When she knew he would not answer she went on, 'Orde will kill you.'

'He might be nervous,' Dawlish argued. 'Benoni could give too much away, so Orde has to find what I want, what I can offer.'

Was it all wishful thinking?

'You're wrong.' Vanessa said softly. 'I can feel it in my bones.' She sat looking at him, almost sultry; not smiling.

'Pat, come away with me, forget Orde and everything else. There's still time. You don't have to throw your life away.' She slid her arms round him. 'Don't go, Pat, don't take a chance.'

He said, 'I'm seeing Orde,' and stood up, forcing himself away from her. She watched him, without expression. He lit another cigarette and drew at it deeply, had nearly finished it before he looked at her. She didn't speak again as they made their way through the great trees towards the car.

No one was near it.

They had coffee and a doughnut at a small restaurant; washed; and then drove slowly along the highway past signs which read *Don't Miss the Meal of Your Life—Stop at the Shoestring*. Part of the way they were clear of the big trees, but they went through another grove of these before the signs for the *Shoestring* grew so huge that no one could have missed them.

They turned a corner and saw the restaurant.

The appointment was in fifteen minutes.

Dawlish drove past, stopped at the first spot where they could pull off the road, and then got out.

'You can come or you can stay here,' he said.

'I'm staying here,' said Vanessa. 'I've taken too many risks for you. I've finished.'

'Leave me the car,' he said dryly.

'You won't need the car again. You won't need anything again.'

He shrugged and turned towards the *Shoestring*. She couldn't have shown more fear if she knew beyond all doubt that death was waiting. She looked pale, too—and she looked so beautiful that it hurt to turn away from her.

He turned.

A big blue Packard pulled off the road. Dawlish caught a glimpse of the two men in it as it passed. They were young, they looked tough, hard, and one of them stared at him. The Packard cut him off from sight of Vanessa. He didn't look round until he was a hundred yards along. The two men stood by the side of the Packard, and Vanessa still sat at the wheel of the old Pontiac.

Dawlish wasn't sure what she would do; wasn't sure about anything.

She might drive on, for she had the money to go alone. She might mean it when she said that she was going to get away so that there was no chance of the police catching up with her. She would be safe in Mexico, probably. She did not appear to suspect that the police might be playing cat and mouse with her.

She might mean anything.

She was smoking and looking towards him, while traffic zoomed past. A huge lumber truck passed, roaring; and when it had gone Dawlish had turned a corner and the girl was out of sight.

So were the two men and the Packard.

The *Shoestring* was just in front of him.

It was a big, log-built restaurant, with a dozen out-houses, a gas station close by, kerb service, everything that one would expect from a big glitter-palace. Over the top was a huge bow, representing a tied shoestring; and although the sun burned down from the clear sky, the thing winked and glittered, yellow, red, blue and green, colours which were washed out by the sun. Few people were about—just two cars.

Dawlish hesitated outside the main door, then went in.

It was very cool inside; almost cold, after the heat of the road. He rubbed his hands together briskly and lit another cigarette. There were several waitresses, in shimmery-looking brown dresses, their hair tied in huge imitation leather bows. None took any notice of him. A man in the same coloured dress, and with a wide shoestring for his tie, stood at the bar at one end of the big room and took no notice of Dawlish either.

There were two families—and a girl, by herself.

Dawlish looked at his watch. It was two minutes over the two hours; time that Orde was here.

No one had fired at him; nothing suggested that Vanessa was right—but he felt on edge. Who wouldn't? He looked at the man, the waitresses and the families, and none of them took the slightest notice of him. That was almost deliberate; as if they meant to turn their backs on a man whom they knew hadn't long to live.

Nonsense?

The girl on her own looked at him and smiled.

She was nice. She wore a lemon-coloured cotton frock and a wisp of tulle round her head, making her face look misty. Her hair was dark brown. She couldn't be more than twenty-two or -three, and that 'nice' expression strengthened as Dawlish looked back at her, and in spite of her smile. She had quite a figure. She was sitting by a window with a cup of coffee in front of her, one hand on the table. Her arms were bare up to halfway between her shoulder and elbow; slim, nicely rounded arms. Her smile might almost be a smile of invitation.

She couldn't be Orde's contact. Could she?

Dawlish went to another table and sat down alone. A waitress came up. He hesitated and then said:

'I'll have coffee and a turkey sandwich, please,' in his most English voice. The girl's eyes widened but she didn't speak; just turned away. One of the families turned, *en masse,* to have a look at him; he couldn't see the other. He lit a cigarette, and began to drum his fingers on the table. Why was everything so slow in happening? Was Orde making sure that he was alone— that there was no trick?

The door opened and two men came in. He had seen them before, and wasn't surprised to see them again. One was tall and dark-haired and smooth-faced, wore a yellow silk blouse, and trousers which were too perfectly pressed; the other was smaller, with a pink shirt and trousers which were too perfectly pressed. They had been in the Packard which had pulled up near Vanessa.

They stared at him.

They walked across the restaurant and opened a door

marked *Private*. It swung to behind them; he could hear the soft, soughing noise as it closed, and the swing grew shorter and shorter.

The nice girl got up.

'Hallo,' she said, by his side, 'you're Patrick Dawlish.'

He didn't answer at once; just looked at her. Until that moment he had been quite sure that the girl was the one person here who could have nothing to do with Orde. Now he was quite sure that she had a job to do with the man. Her eyes were brown, and they smiled—as her lips smiled. One could take a look at Vanessa and sense the danger, the capacity for evil; but one would not dream that such capacity lay in this girl.

'May I sit down?' she asked, and slid into the seat opposite him. For the first time he noticed that she wore a wedding ring.

'Sure,' he said dryly.

Her eyes glowed.

'You're very kind. You were punctual.'

'I like to be. Where's . . .' He didn't finish.

'You didn't expect Orde to be here in person, did you?' Her eyes mocked him.

'Yes,' he said, slowly and deliberately.

'Oh, *no*,' she said. 'He wants you to go and see him. I'm to take you to the lumber mill.'

'If he wants to see Benoni again,' Dawlish said, 'he can come and talk to me here. I'm not going to the lumber mill until I've talked to Orde.' He smiled and thrust cigarettes towards her. 'Smoke?'

'No, thanks, I never smoke.' She didn't stop smiling, but there wasn't quite the same confidence in her manner. 'You'll have to go, Mr. Dawlish.'

He grinned at her.

The waitress brought his coffee. He was tempted to say that he wanted it after the sandwich, but didn't. He sipped it slowly. Then the sandwich was brought.

'Will you join me?' he asked gravely.

'No, thanks,' she said. Her voice was husky, and he was sure that she didn't come from this part of the United States; he would have heard a voice like it on the East Coast more often than here. But in her quiet way she was good-looking. There were two small brown moles on her right cheek. The right word for her was 'restful'. In spite of his pose, he hadn't really recovered from the shock of knowing that she was from Orde.

'You'll have to come with me,' she said.

'Sorry, sweetheart. Go back and tell him that I'm more obstinate than one of the black bears.'

She didn't speak.

He ate the sandwich and finished the coffee—and then suddenly yawned. It caught him completely by surprise. He wasn't tired; not tired to a point of exhaustion, not so tired that he ought to be caught out by a yawn. That stabbed through him—and with it came the first real fears.

The girl was *laughing* at him.

'Look—' he began thickly.

'Don't worry,' she said. 'He really wants to talk to you.' She stretched out a hand and touched his as he struggled to get up. He couldn't. His knees were wobbly, his whole body was suddenly weak. He looked down at her face. It seemed to be going round and round, and instead of being so sweet and friendly and 'nice' there was a satyrish look about it. *Satyrish?*

He sat down heavily.

The door marked *Private* opened and the two smooth-looking, sleekly dressed men came and headed straight for him.

No one else took the slightest notice. He opened his mouth—
and another yawn took hold of him.

He felt hazy—as if he were blacking out.

He *was* blacking out.

CHAPTER XVI

ORDE

Dawlish heard sounds.

He did not recognize them—but they were there, like a swarm of bees humming viciously inside his head. They wouldn't stop. His head ached, but he knew that it would be better if only there were no buzzing.

He got used to it.

He was bound hand and foot.

He remembered everything that had happened, including the near panic when he had felt blackness falling about him. Now, he could use his mind. If they wanted to kill him they would kill, not dope him. The fact that they had doped him was a hopeful sign—wasn't it?

Soon he would see Orde.

If only that buzzing would stop; buzzing as if it were coming from a dozen giant saws at the same time.

He was nearer Orde than he had ever been; soon he would be talking to the man; soon he would know whether there was a chance to find out what he desperately wanted to know.

There *had* to be a chance. He would have to make one.

He felt himself go shivery.

Was that the after-effects of the dope? Or general weakness? Or excitement? There had been a time when there had seemed no possibility at all of coming face to face with Orde. Now it might be only a matter of minutes before the door opened and the man came in.

Damn that buzzing!

Suddenly it stopped.

At first he could hardly believe it. The silence was like a vacuum. There had been the buzzing of the million of angry bees; or dozens of huge saws; and now there was silence. In fact there was a whining sound which gradually faded; then the silence came.

He looked about him.

He could just see the outline of the window and knew that it was still daylight. He had no idea what kind of a room this was—but it began to dawn on him that he was actually at the lumber mill, that he had heard the circular saws buzzing as they cut through the redwood trunks.

He found himself on edge, in case they started up again. They didn't. He heard men moving about outside and voices; but they passed.

Then he heard footsteps, swift and brisk—those of a woman. Were they coming nearer? He held his breath, because it mattered so much.

The sound changed; the footsteps echoed as if on boards; and the room shook. She was coming up wooden steps towards the room. He stared at the vague outline of the door, and then heard a key, a creaking sound—and daylight flooded the room where he lay.

The girl came in alone. First a frame-mesh door, then one of solid wood, closed behind her.

It was dark again, but soon she had the window open, although there was a frame of wire mesh beyond, to keep out insects. The light wasn't so harsh. She was dressed now in a cream-coloured blouse and a skirt. She looked fresh and lovely.

'Hi,' she said. 'How are you feeling?'

'I'm—wonderful,' he growled.

She laughed and came across to him, looking down. Her brown eyes seemed too lovely for anyone who could possibly work for Orde. He saw her wedding ring again.

'That's fine.' She had a pocket in her skirt and took something out—a knife. Dawlish stared at it. A knife in the hands of a man might have scared him, but in her slim, pale fingers it seemed—diabolic. He couldn't keep his gaze away. The blade flashed. She knew exactly what she was going to do, hadn't a moment's hesitation.

She cut something close to his sides; he felt the tension at his wrists ease.

'Don't do anything silly, Mr. Dawlish,' she said. 'The shack is watched. If you try to escape you'll be shot.' She said that quite calmly. 'You can move about the room, and do what you like in here.'

'Where's Orde?' he asked.

'He'll see you.'

'*Where is he?*'

'He'll see you,' she repeated, and turned away and went out, as if she hadn't much time or patience for him. He watched the door close, and apparently she made no attempt to lock it.

He sat up.

He was in a large room with rough log walls, a rough-hewn table, two rocking-chairs, oddments of furniture, cupboards, stools. The floor was spread with three black bear rugs. On the table there were whisky—bourbon—soda—and even a jug

144

of ice, as if they didn't mean him to go without anything he needed.

The worst of it all was the unexpectedness.

He was very stiff.

He moved around the room several times, until his legs felt more like his own and his arms also felt as if they belonged to him. Then he poured himself a drink. As he drank he thought of the possibility that the bourbon was poisoned—and then couldn't think of any reason why they should poison it now; so he let himself enjoy it.

He went to the door.

He hesitated for a moment and then opened it. He narrowed his eyes against the brilliance of the setting sun. The door faced west; and soon the sun would drop below the tops of the trees.

Four wooden steps led down to the clearing; there were no trees within fifty yards of the shack itself. A few great stumps were within easy reach. It appeared to be at the top of a hill, but because of the trees he couldn't see beyond.

The trees were vast.

They stood packed together too, as if defying anyone or anything to push them over; yet not far away was a saw, and the great giants could be felled in a few hours. He found himself thinking of that vaguely; comparing himself with the trees themselves—his puny weakness and their puny might.

He saw men standing among the trees—counted three in all, watching him. The girl had warned him about them. He wondered what would happen if he started to walk about the clearing. They wouldn't let him get away, but—he didn't *want* to get away. He had to see Orde and to fool Orde, and find the truth. That was all-important.

Then he heard a sound at a corner of the shack.

A man came in sight—big, thickset, needing a shave. There

were men who seemed made to fit the word 'tough' and he was one of them. He carried an axe. In the hands of most men it would have looked enormous, but in his it was little more than a chopper.

He stood at the foot of the four steps staring at Dawlish—then suddenly and without the slightest warning he lifted the axe *and flung it.*

One moment Dawlish stood staring at him.

Next Dawlish saw the movements of that huge body, saw the axe glitter in the slanting rays of the sun, saw it hurtling towards him.

He knew fear as he had seldom known it.

He ducked.

The axe hurtled over his head and smashed against the far wall. The shack shook violently. Something fell. The man who had thrown it grinned at him slowly; and Dawlish was reminded suddenly of the great black bear which had stood close to him when he had driven away from the beach, leaving Victor and his companion by themselves.

'Get inside,' the man said.

He moved forward.

Dawlish backed away. The man followed. His movements were slow and deliberate; ponderous. He seemed to fill the doorway. Normally his size would not have worried Dawlish. His physical strength wouldn't have worried him anyhow; but something did now. It was as if the man had come here to terrify him, and for once he was easy to frighten.

The man shot out his hand, thrust Dawlish back and brought him up against the wall, sharply, painfully. He banged the back of his head. Then the man stalked towards the wall where the axe was biting deep into the rough logs.

He took it out, wrenching it this way and that to get it free, and then turned. With the same sudden, vicious movement, displaying a strength which seemed hardly human, he hurled the axe out of the doorway. It hurtled through the air and came to rest on one of the tree-stumps; it stuck there, quivering.

He chuckled.

The odd thing about the man was his slowness, except in those swift, violent, twisting turns; and, until that moment, his silence. The chuckle was hoarse, animal. His little blue eyes shone, as if he were thoroughly enjoying himself. He turned and moved towards Dawlish, slowly, head on one side and arms thrust out. His hand was spread wide. Obviously he was going to pin Dawlish against the wall.

Dawlish felt the mists of weakness in his back, his legs, his arms. He knew that it was because of the drug; he knew that he shouldn't feel like this.

The man seemed to hypnotize him.

The great hand drew nearer, and touched his chest, then pushed him slowly, remorselessly, against the wall. He couldn't help himself. He wanted—above everything else, he wanted—to fight back, but he knew in that moment that he couldn't. He had to give way. The walls were hard against his back, grinding into his shoulder-blades; the pressure of the hand at his chest was like that of a giant drill, pressing, twisting this way and that as if to bore a hole through him. The pain was bad at first, and grew worse. He clenched his teeth; it was difficult not to shout out because of the pain.

The pressure eased.

'Ach,' the giant said, and slapped him across the face. It was like a buffet with a spade, set Dawlish's head ringing, made him stagger to one side. The man spat at him and the spittle caught the side of his face. 'Ach,' he said again, and turned and lumbered out.

Dawlish was left alone, with his own harsh breathing for company; that and the pain at his chest and the weakness and the knowledge that he hadn't lifted a finger to protect himself.

He moved slowly.

He pressed his hands against his forehead and went across to the table. The thing that had fallen was the thick glass. He picked it up. He saw the great cut where the axe had bitten into the log—it had split it in two. If that blade had struck his head his skull would have been split open in a trice. Knife through butter wasn't in it. The man *could* have aimed at his head; or, as bad, hit him by accident. Dawlish studied the split log with a stupid kind of application.

Then he poured himself another drink, without worrying about the ice.

He turned towards the open door, glass in hand.

A man stood there; and he knew in a moment that it was Orde, although he had never seen Orde in his life.

'Just imagine what could happen to you if you tried to make a monkey out of me,' Orde said. 'He could split your skull in two—or break every bone you've got. Remember that.'

Orde was tall, but not massive like the brute. He was middle-aged, with iron-grey hair, cut close. He wasn't a handsome man, but he gave an impression of strength. His faced was lined, less with age than with the weather; and stiff with a kind of tension. It was a smooth-shaven face, the features small and very sharp; the nose might have been an eagle's beak, carved out of rock.

Dawlish watched his eyes.

They were grey. His back was to the light, and they were partly in shadow, but their brilliance showed. If eyes could frighten, the eyes of this man could.

He wore an open-necked shirt, grey trousers, high-heeled boots; as if he had been riding.

'Where's Benoni, Dawlish?' he asked.

There was the rather high-pitched, unusual voice, which wasn't quite real. It placed him as surely as his appearance; as everything else about him.

'Forget it,' Dawlish said, and was glad that he could find words. 'You and I have to talk before Benoni—'

Orde said, 'Where's Benoni, Dawlish?' He spoke as if Dawlish had said nothing—as if Dawlish couldn't have heard the question. That, in a sentence, explained the man; he took it for granted that he would be answered and that the answer would be the truth; he would not allow the possibility that anyone would refuse to answer.

'Forget Benoni,' Dawlish said with great care. He had to speak carefully. His chest hurt where the pressure of that huge hand had bruised him; and his arms, legs and back were still weak. 'After we've talked—'

Orde turned on his heel. He was one of those men who moved very gracefully—as animals moved. Stealthily. He did not worry because his back was turned towards Dawlish, but went out again and called:

'Kurt!'

'Yeh, boss,' a man said; and the hoarse voice told Dawlish that it was the bear-like brute who had attacked him once.

He was nearby.

'I want to make him talk,' Orde said. 'Get busy.'

He moved aside; and the man named Kurt came up the wooden steps. He parted his lips. They were red and they looked moist and he licked them.

CHAPTER XVII

THE FIGHT

Orde did not go far.

Dawlish saw the big man darken the doorway, and because the sun had now fallen below the level of the trees it was much duller here than it had been. Then Orde stepped forward and actually came inside the shack.

The man named Kurt drew nearer. Dawlish noticed his long arms, which were almost to his knees. He already knew about the tremendous strength, and he could see the matt of black and greying hair at the V of the check shirt. He saw the moist, red lips. He knew that Kurt was out to enjoy himself—and he knew that it wouldn't matter to Orde if he broke every bone in Dawlish's body.

Kurt seemed to take it for granted that he could hypnotize Dawlish; that Dawlish wouldn't move.

It was almost a form of hypnotism.

The great hands stretched out for Dawlish's neck; and then at the last moment Dawlish screwed himself up to effort and moved to one side. He didn't go as swiftly as he wanted to—his body was behind his mind. He felt the hands brush against him.

Then, with one of those fantastically swift movements, Kurt turned and clutched again.

His hands gripped. Dawlish felt the vice-like power of the great fingers.

Dawlish clenched his fists and drove them into Kurt's stomach. He hadn't much room, but both fists struck home at the same time. He heard the breath driven out of the big man's body. The fingers slackened. He dodged to one side—and this time he moved swiftly enough. Kurt didn't get him when he grabbed again.

Dawlish glanced at Orde.

Orde was *smiling*.

There wasn't any time to look at Orde for long. Dawlish watched Kurt. The blow had warned Kurt that this wasn't going to be as easy as he expected. He stood quite still, hands working. Dawlish was closer to the wall, opposite the door. The door offered a way of escape, but it would only be temporary escape. The battle would be settled here.

Kurt leapt.

Dawlish turned, twisted, shot out a foot, kicked against Kurt's shins, then shoved him with all the strength he could find. Kurt smashed against the wall. He didn't like it, and he grunted with the pain; a bear couldn't have sounded more bestial. He swung round and came again. Dawlish shot out a straight to the chin and touched, but it was like hitting a piece of iron. That didn't matter; what mattered was keeping Kurt at arm's length. Those great arms could crush him if they got too close.

Dawlish caught a glimpse of the doorway.

Other men were outside now; and Orde stood there, with that grin on his smooth face—the kind of grin a man might show if he were enjoying himself.

Forget Orde.

Kurt stood some feet away, crouching, arms stretched forward, lips parted, breath coming in uneven gasps. He hadn't expected this, and didn't like it. Dawlish dashed the sweat out of his eyes and waited—and knew that he shouldn't wait, time was against him. Normally, he might have hoped to stay the course, but not this day; there was that weakness everywhere, and he was very conscious of it.

Kurt sprang.

Dawlish saw the flexing of the muscles just in time; the speed of the other's great body was fantastic. Dawlish whirled round. A hand struck the side of his head, his head rang, he knew that he couldn't take any more like that—and it had been only a glancing blow.

Kurt staggered past him.

Dawlish turned and leapt, grabbed the left arm, twisted, heard the sudden slobbering breath as pain shot through Kurt's arm. Nothing mattered but putting Kurt out of action—*nothing*. Kurt stood half crouching, fighting against the pressure at his arm, knowing what would happen if he struggled too furiously. His head was twisted, hate showed in his eyes. Dawlish twisted; put all the strength he could into that. The arm should break; no man should be able to stand up to such pressure, but Kurt did. Dawlish felt the sweat gather on his forehead and face, heard himself gasping for breath. . . .

Then the crack came.

Kurt squealed, and all resistance went. The big body was like a jelly. Dawlish let him go and pushed. Kurt staggered towards the door, couldn't save himself, and fell. The shack shook. He tried to get up, but there was pain in his eyes, and there was nothing he could do. Men at the door came rushing in, one of them with a knife in his hand.

Dawlish saw him.

Dawlish saw Orde staring, still smiling; lasciviously. He had enjoyed seeing that fight, had enjoyed the crack of the breaking bone.

Dawlish turned his back on the man with the knife and on Orde, and went slowly to the table and poured himself a drink. It didn't matter what happened now, he would not be able to defend himself. Every ounce of strength had been spent on that fantastic struggle; and he could still hardly believe that he had won.

Orde said, 'Leave him.'

The man with the knife was close to Dawlish. He stopped moving. Dawlish turned and looked at him, sipping his drink. Two others were helping Kurt to his feet; soon they disappeared into the gathering gloom. Not far off there was a wood fire burning; Dawlish smelt the acrid fumes and could see the firelight. He finished his drink. He had little strength left, so little that Orde could have pushed him over. He would be better in half an hour, if he were allowed the time in which to rest.

He took out cigarettes.

'So you're strong,' Orde said.

'That's right,' said Dawlish. 'Next time, someone will get hurt.' He lit the cigarette. 'You're a difficult man to convince Orde, but perhaps you'll agree that I don't waste words.

'So you don't.'

'Why make yourself so hard to talk to?' asked Dawlish.

'I know just who you are, what you want. I know everything,' Orde said. He spoke so calmly that he sounded as if he believed it; in a way, he did believe it. 'You worked for M.I.5, and you were named as a traitor and Haffmeyer and others put a finger on you. Why should I talk to you?'

Dawlish said: 'You've got a reputation. You buy secret information, and I've got plenty and know how to get more. I can't help it if you're just another fool, ready to throw a fortune away.'

He was glad of the cigarette. He sat on a corner of the table, and hoped that he didn't betray the fact that he was physically beaten. The light was poor, and hid the greyness of his cheeks. He was suffering from reaction and needed everything he had got to keep his voice steady. But this was the angle; persuade Orde that he would work with him, come to terms until such time as he learned why Orde had paid Haffmeyer to brand him—*if* Orde had.

'So I'm a fool.' Orde seemed amused. 'Supposing you're still with M.I.5, Dawlish.'

Dawlish said, 'If they could catch me, they'd kill me.'

Orde mocked, 'They don't do that kind of thing in England; you would have to stand trial.'

Dawlish laughed. He was proud of that laugh. It came suddenly and was certainly the last thing that Orde would expect. He shifted his position and said:

'So you think the English are soft, too?'

'Ever heard of people like Nunn May?'

'Ever heard of people who die by accident?' Dawlish asked softly. 'Orde, I was framed. I didn't cheat M.I.5. But they believed a no-good like Haffmeyer, and they made me hate their guts. They won't worry about a trial. They'll make it an accidental death. If it came to a point, they'd make it murder. They know I know too much. They're afraid that I'll sell out to the highest bidder.'

He gave the laugh again.

'How right they are!' he said.

'You're lying,' Orde said, but there wasn't the same confidence in his voice. Dawlish half wished that the light were better, so that he could see the man's face and expression. Outside it was nearly dark, and the flickering light of the fire showed much more clearly.

Orde said abruptly, 'What have you got to sell?'

'For years I've been close to the big shots in M.I.5,' Dawlish said. 'For years there's been nothing they wouldn't trust me with. I've plenty—stored up there.' He touched his head. 'If anything happened to stop that from working, it would stop me from telling what I know. And *torture* won't do it, Orde, not now or at any time. I want to cash in, then lose myself somewhere. That's what I wanted to see you about. That's why I've taken the risks.'

'Why did you go to see Haffmeyer?'

'To find out who he worked for—to find a buyer for my information. He was killed before he could talk.'

'Vanessa kill him?' It seemed a genuine question—but surely Orde knew the killer.

'She says she didn't.'

Orde grinned.

'Who'd believe her? And who'd believe *you*? Haffmeyer was ready to squeal on me. He had worked for me for years. You were going to soften him up, but you hadn't time. The F.B.I. were after him, too. That man Kell you saw was going to learn all that Haffmeyer could tell him about.'

Dawlish said: 'Haffmeyer had put a finger on me, and finished me with M.I.5. I needed money, and I thought he could put me on to a buyer. That's all.'

At least Orde was listening.

'Who else knew that Haffmeyer worked for me?'

'I didn't, until after he was dead. Victor talked—and Vanessa had heard Haffmeyer talk of you.'

'That the truth?' Orde barked.

Dawlish stubbed his cigarette out on a saucer.

'It's true. I've been looking for you because I think we could do a deal, Orde. You've got the one thing I want.'

'What's that?'

'Money.'

Orde didn't speak.

'I can use money,' Dawlish said. 'I've a lot to sell. Information about M.I.5, and British Government secrets and plenty about Anglo-American espionage liaison; plenty. It's just a question of agreeing a price.' He lit another cigarette. 'Where is Vanessa?'

'Forget her.'

'Listen, Orde,' Dawlish said, and his voice cracked. 'You don't seem to know the kind of deal you can make with me. I'm here to talk terms—and when I ask questions I want answers. I'll tell you one thing I did—'

He paused.

Orde took a step forward. He hadn't smoked; he hadn't had a drink. Now it was almost dark, and outside the red firelight from the unseen fire glowed and made the night warm and friendly; it even showed the massive trunks of the distant trees. Yet Orde's face was in darkness, and the only thing that Dawlish could see was the glitter of his eyes.

He didn't come too near.

'What did you do?'

Dawlish said, 'I wrote a letter to an F.B.I. agent who is looking for me—Exton, at Eureka.' Orde would know that there was such a man up the coast, and that he was F.B.I. 'I told him where to find Benoni. I arranged for that letter to be delivered by tomorrow night. To make sure nothing went wrong with it I also arranged for a telephone message to be sent to Exton from a restaurant. Now Benoni can tell plenty, Orde—so you and me had better agree on a deal in time to get Benoni away from his hiding-place before Exton finds him.'

He took the cigarette from his lips.

'Where's Vanessa?' he asked. 'Vanessa isn't to be hurt—understand?'

CHAPTER XVIII

TEMPTATION

There was no way of being sure that he had won himself a chance. He believed that he had; but that might mean nothing. He wished Orde would speak. He wished there were light. He wanted to get out of the shack and into the night, for there would be people near the fire—other people who would talk, whose eyes wouldn't glitter like Orde's.

He knew what it was to feel frightened of Orde.

Orde said, 'Vanessa's okay.'

'So you picked her up?'

'You can take it from me I picked her up,' Orde said, and there seemed to be a faint laugh in his voice. What mattered was that he was talking, making concessions. 'I've had a little talk with Vanessa. She isn't feeling so good.'

Dawlish felt his mouth go dry.

'What have you done to her?'

'You can go and see for yourself,' Orde said. 'She's in the next shack. The door isn't locked. This way.'

He moved towards the door. He made little sound, and although Dawlish could see only a shadowy shape he sensed that the man still moved with animal grace. Then suddenly other shapes appeared; not human. Two great dogs came up and snuffed about Dawlish, and then stood in front of Orde. There was dull light from the fire, but Dawlish couldn't be sure what breed these were.

'If you try to get away,' Orde said, 'they'll tear you to bits.'

Dawlish said sharply, 'I came to see you, didn't I?'

They walked down the steps, Dawlish imagined there were other shapes, other dogs and men. He saw the fire, some distance off among the trees, and several men sat round it. He followed Orde. There was another shack, just a dark silhouette, nearby. It looked identical with the one in which Dawlish had been.

'You can go and see her,' Orde said. 'Just remember—don't try to run away.'

Dawlish said: 'You're chasing shadows. I want to be here.'

He made out the shape of the other shack, went up the steps and opened the door. At first he wondered if it would be locked, if Orde were fooling him; but why should Orde fool him in little things? He found that the door opened freely. It was dark. He heard a rustle of movement, and then the sharp intake of breath. He stood outlined against the door for a second, then struck a match. It shone on him, not on whoever was here.

'Who—who is it?' That was Vanessa.

Dawlish turned in the light and saw an electric switch, pressed it down, and then looked across at the corner where Vanessa lay on a couch. It was a room very like the other, but better furnished, much more comfortable; and there were settees and easy chairs. Vanessa lay on the largest couch, knees drawn up. She had no make-up on. Her eyes were swollen. There were red patches on her cheeks. Her clothes were torn. One stocking was laddered a dozen times, from knee to ankle; and there were scratches on her arm.

She said in a thin voice: 'Pat for *Patrick*. If you knew how I hate the *sight* of you.'

He closed the door.

'What did they do?'

'What *didn't* they do?' She was savage. The light was in the centre of the room and made shadows of her face. Much of her beauty was hidden. She sat up more comfortably; he thought that she had been dozing. Her hair was crushed on one side. If she glanced into the mirror she would probably dislike him even more.

He said: 'I'm sorry, Van.'

'I told you what would happen!'

'It hasn't happened yet.'

'If you think Orde will ever let us get away from here you're crazy,' she said; there was weariness rather than spite in her voice; and a kind of hopelessness.

'Orde and I can do a deal. What did they want from you?'

She didn't answer at first, but gradually the story came. They had questioned her about what he, Dawlish, had said; they had wanted every detail of their conversations. Now and again, to encourage her, she said they had slapped her and pulled her hair and pushed her about.

She had told them everything—that Dawlish wanted to do a deal with Orde, why he had come; but she hadn't told them where Benoni was.

Dawlish watched her, still wondering; quite dispassionate. Her colour was better, she didn't look so sick now. 'I told them nearly everything I could,' she said.

'You did fine,' he said slowly. 'Cigarette?' She took one and drew at the smoke. He looked round the shack and saw a cupboard, went to it and found bourbon and everything needed for a drink. He mixed one, then bent down, kissed her lightly on the lips, gave her the drink and went to the door. He put out the light, then said:

'I'll make sure Orde doesn't beat you up any more.'

'*You'll* make sure!' she sneered.

He shrugged and went out. A dark shape loomed up out of the gloom, and he felt his heart leap, it was one of the dogs.

He wondered what game Orde was playing. M.I.5 would like to know, but for the time being that was secondary. In clearing himself, he would put M.I.5 on to Orde.

He wondered what tests Orde would think up.

He did not go straight to his shack, but towards the fire. It was a hundred yards away, through the trees. He saw the silhouettes of men against it. As he drew nearer, he saw more; there was a great circular saw close to it, in an open shed—a roof on big stakes. The saw was enormous. He knew what had caused the buzzing sound as he saw the firelight shine red on the sharp teeth.

He was hungry.

He didn't join the men by the fire, because there were so many of them, but Orde wasn't among them. He turned away. Now he could see much better. His only company were the two dogs, shapes which were close to him all the time, but which he couldn't hear.

This was as if Orde were giving him a chance to try to escape; the simple tricks would come first.

He went back towards the shack and then in. He hadn't noticed an electric light switch when he had been in it before; but as there was one in Vanessa's, why not a light in here? He didn't strike a match, but groped for the switch in the same position as it had been in Vanessa's shack.

He found it, and light came on.

'Hi,' said the girl from the *Shoestring*.

* * *

She wore the blouse and the skirt, looked so fresh and young—demure, that was the word—that she made Dawlish stand and stare at her. She wrinkled up her nose at him.

'Shut the door,' she said, 'you'll have all the flies and mosquitoes in.'

He could hear them humming.

He let the frame-door close, and then walked forward. The other door swung to. The girl was standing by the table, which had been laid for a meal. There was a damask table-cloth on it, and glittering cutlery, a chicken, some ham, salad, everything anyone would want for a cold meal. On a small table nearby were some cans of beer; and there was iced water. She looked away from him to run an experienced eye over the table, and said:

'Salt, where's that, now?'

She turned and opened the door of a cupboard behind her; found the salt, and put it on the table.

'Hungry?'

'Famished.'

'That's good, so am I.'

'Orde decided that I don't have to starve to death?'

She said: 'Pat, why don't you count your blessings as they come? Sit down. And I've a name—Alice.' Her eyes laughed at him, and she pushed up a chair. Two places were laid, and she took the other. Then, in the most business-like way, she set about carving the chicken.

It was good. . . .

Everything was good, for the moment; he could believe in the future again.

'Has Vanessa plenty to eat?' he asked.

'Yes,' the girl named Alice said, and shot him an unexpectedly serious look from those brown eyes. 'Vanessa's okay.' She went on eating for a few minutes, but the subject was obviously still on her mind. She started it again. 'Vanessa was your big mistake.'

'How?'

'He doesn't trust her. He never has trusted her. If she had said something different from what you said, it would have been better. He can't believe that she would ever tell the truth. See how I mean?'

'It's his mind,' Dawlish said. 'Warped.'

'Don't be funny about Orde.'

'No,' Dawlish said soberly, 'you've got something there. Vanessa's told him the truth because she's too frightened not to.'

Alice was staring at him.

'*Have* you told Orde the truth?' She couldn't really believe it.

'Every word.'

'He'll find out if you've lied,' she said, and suddenly jumped up. 'I'll get some coffee.'

There was some on a hot-plate; she brought it to the table and poured out; she pushed a bowl of wrapped sugar towards him. The light shone on the chased platinum of her wedding ring.

'Don't make any mistake,' she said. 'Orde—' She stopped; he thought that she shivered. 'He *knows* when people are lying to him. It's a kind of sixth sense. I've known people who believe that they get away with lies, but in the end he always gets them.'

She paused.

He knew that this was all part of the game; all part of Orde's high-pressuring, and the fact that it was done too smoothly and so gently made it more dangerous. It was dangerous because she was so demure and appealing and seemed genuinely anxious to help him.

She said abruptly: 'He hates liars. He'll punish liars more than he'll punish anyone. *Pat, have you lied to him?*'

'No,' he said. 'There's no reason why I should lie. I'm on the spot. He might get me off it—no one else will.'

He lit a cigarette, after she had refused; and he remembered that Orde didn't smoke, either. 'I don't propose to lie to Orde or to anyone. I don't like him but I admire him.' He grinned. 'I would admire anyone who could make you loyal!'

She didn't smile.

'We serve the same ideals,' she said, quite soberly.

He knew, as surely as he was sitting here, why she had said it. She wanted the question to come, '*What ideals*?' This was part of the trick to find out what he really wanted, to probe into his mind, to find out his beliefs. Orde knew he was no traitor; Orde might suspect his real reason for coming and the girl might simply have the task of trying to bring his real thoughts to the surface. She was the temptress and her demure beauty made her dangerous; deadly.

'He said, 'That's the first thing that's worried me.'

'What do you mean?' she asked swiftly, and watched him.

'I can trust a man who's bad for money; I can trust a man who's just bad; but trusting an *idealist* . . .' He pushed his chair back, stood up and gave the sharp laugh which had once startled Orde. 'Now I'm really worried,' he said, but he grinned down at her. 'Where is he, do you know?'

CHAPTER XIX

NEW IDEA?

As he spoke, Dawlish watched the girl. The thing that surprised him was the look of disbelief, almost of horror, in her eyes. She tried to hide it, but it was there. She turned away before he had finished speaking, but still couldn't rid him of the impression she had created.

She was *serious.*

He went on roughly:

'Orde sells out to the highest bidder, that's what's in it for him. Let's get rid of the cant. I don't give a damn who buys it; what I want is a cut in whatever Orde gets for what I can tell him.'

He lit a cigarette.

'I see,' she said. He got the impression again that she was shaken, *and that she was disappointed.* That came afterwards, dawning slowly, and he didn't like it. The trouble was that the girl was so nice—pleasant—candid. It had always been difficult to associate her with the evil that he knew to be in Orde; and it was more difficult now.

'He'll come when he's ready,' she said. 'Don't forget what I told you, Mr. Dawlish. He cannot be deceived and he dislikes lying more than most things.'

'Being the soul of rectitude himself,' sneered Dawlish.

She turned on him suddenly. She caught her breath, as if something hurt her; next moment she was just in front of him, her eyes blazing, her hands raised in front of her high breasts. Her cheeks were pale but the brilliance of her eyes made it easy to forget that.

'Do you think it's easy for him?' she breathed. 'Do you think he *enjoys* using men like Haffmeyer and Kurt and all these brutes? Do you think he likes bribing and tricking and cheating? He does it because it's the only way. Understand, there just isn't any other way!'

She swung round and went out. First one then the other door clanged behind her. He stood staring at them—forgetting that he stared at blank wood. He could see the girl's face in his mind's eye, with all the fury of indignation which had so startled him.

Her fury, her outburst, the storm of indignation, squared with her general manner; nothing else did. She didn't square with Orde, who could instruct a brute like Kurt to soften a man up so that the man would talk.

Dawlish finished his cigarette and began to move round the room. He didn't quite know why he wouldn't go outside. It wasn't fear; he hadn't intended to try to escape before, and escape was much further from his mind now.

Were there factors involved of which he hadn't dreamt? Until now, he had at least felt certain that Orde was bad; a renegade; a spy above all spies.

Crazy!

There couldn't be any doubt about that.

He lit another cigarette, then turned towards the door. He

would go out, and probably have only the dogs for company. He might go and see Vanessa; she—

He heard footsteps, and then the door opened. Orde came in. Dawlish wasn't really surprised even by Orde's appearance. He was pale—or he looked pale. Dawlish reminded himself that this was the first time he had seen the man in a good light. The pallor was unexpected; the eyes still glittered. The lines were there, and the strangeness of the face—he didn't look natural.

His voice wasn't natural, either.

Watching him, Dawlish realized one thing which had been hinted at before: the man looked more like a mechanical creature, not of flesh and blood. The girl was real enough; so was Vanessa; so was Benoni; but if he were told that this were an animated wax model, he wouldn't be wholly incredulous.

'Hallo,' Dawlish said. 'Smoke?'

Orde shook his head. He had one hand in his pocket, the other by his side.

'I want to know what you can tell me,' he said, 'and want to know the price.'

Dawlish was so taken aback that he didn't answer.

'Quickly!' snapped Orde. 'I'm in a hurry.'

Dawlish watched him; he knew that it wouldn't do to wait too long, the man was eaten up with impatience; that was because he was so used to having his own way, doing exactly what he wanted. But Dawlish needed a respite; needed time to get over the shock of what looked like complete capitulation.

Could it be?

Orde drew a deep breath. '*Quickly!*'

Dawlish began. . . .

He told the story that he had carefully prepared—the story which was to satisfy Orde that he had become a renegade. He knew it off by heart. He was sure that he wouldn't make a single mistake in the wording, but—could he tell it as if it were the truth, as if there were no possibility that he was lying? Could he fool Orde? Was there any sense in the girl's story that this man could smell out the truth?

Dawlish used a low-pitched, level voice; kept off all emotion; now and again hesitated, as if he were having to force himself to go on. It was the kind of behaviour one might expect from a man who was doing what he knew he shouldn't; a man who was betraying those things to which he should be loyal. All the time Orde stood and watched with those burning eyes, as if he were trying to pierce Dawlish's mind, as if he could see the truth beneath this carefully prepared series of lies and half-truths.

He could supply drawings and plans of the latest guided missiles, the latest guided aircraft, new fuels, germ warfare, tanks, submarines. Everything that he might be expected to know he claimed to know. It was a long list. He covered every detail, and he explained in some cases how he had managed to get hold of them. Everything, even the tone of his voice, had to be convincing.

There came a time when he knew that he would have to stop; when he would have to give Orde a chance to say something, and when he would know whether Orde believed him or not. He couldn't postpone the moment for long, but the nearer it drew, the more he feared it.

Then he finished:

'Now I need a buyer, Orde, a big money man.'

He took out cigarettes, but didn't light one. He looked into those burning eyes and tried to persuade himself that he hadn't made a single mistake, that Orde would have to believe him, the story was so obviously true.

'Where's all this information and how can I be sure it's genuine?' Orde asked sharply.

'It's hidden where I can put my hands on it whenever I like,' Dawlish said. 'It isn't all in the same place.'

'You in this alone?'

'Yes.'

'What about your wife?'

Dawlish kept a poker face.

'There are things that can't be helped,' he said. 'I had to leave her.'

'Any idea of getting together again?'

Dawlish lit his cigarette, watching the man closely, hoping that he wasn't overplaying his hand. There were questions in his mind which worried him. Just what was Orde after? Was he half convinced or was he fooling Dawlish—was this cat and mouse? There was cruelty in the man's face; no, that wasn't it, there was a quality of inhumanity. The impression that Orde wasn't real, wasn't human, came again, much more strongly.

Dawlish answered: 'M.I.5 will watch my wife as if she mattered more than anything else in the world. Every move she makes, everywhere she goes, everyone she sees, everyone she telephones, will be known. They'll keep it up for years; they'll probably keep it up for ever. So there isn't any way of getting my wife back. That was one of the things I weighed up before I started out on this.'

Orde said quickly: 'Okay, okay. You haven't told me how I can be sure the stuff is genuine.'

'You haven't given me much time. You can see some of it in advance. Not the biggest stuff and not all of it, but enough to check. You've your own scientists, haven't you? Your own physicists. You can check.'

'Never mind what I've got,' Orde said. 'Where do I find it?'

'We've got to agree a price,' Dawlish reminded him softly.

'Before we do anything else, we have to agree a price. Don't let's have any doubt about that.'

'Name your price.'

Dawlish drew harder at his cigarette. He let the other stare at him, as if trying to bore a way into his thoughts. He had a strange, sickening feeling, something like the one he had known before the fight with Kurt—but worse. His heart thumped. He believed now that Orde took his word for part of this; that Orde could be fooled. They would come to terms; Orde would be off his guard. What then? Find proof that he had paid Haffmeyer to lie, and find out why.

On the way here Dawlish had been driven by the belief that he could win; now that he was here he found himself fearful of ultimate failure. He could break Orde, but could he save himself?

'Name your price!' Orde insisted.

Dawlish said: 'All right. Vanessa, free and unhurt. A guaranteed safe conduct to Mexico. Then a deal between you and me, as individuals; no third parties, no one else nearby to pull a fast one on me. And—all the dope I've got for a million dollars in cash. That's all.'

The other's eyes were like burning coals.

Dawlish had never felt more like turning away; never felt it so difficult to meet a man's gaze. He remembered what the girl had said of Orde: that he could divine a lie. Looking at Orde, Dawlish began to feel that it was true.

The silence dragged out.

Then:

'I'll think it over,' Orde said. 'Where are these samples?'

Very slowly, Dawlish said, 'In the heel of my right shoe.' He sat down on a rocking-chair and it tossed him gently to and fro. He kicked off his right shoe. Orde made no attempt to draw nearer. Dawlish lifted the shoe, took out a penknife and prised; and part of the heel moved outwards, revealing a tiny cavity inside. He probed, and pulled out some tiny rolls of paper; he put three on his knee, and then shook out two more. He held them out to Orde, closed the heel of the shoe and put the shoe on again.

'How long will you be making up your mind?' he asked.

'Two or three days,' Orde said. He stared down at the rolls as if he could not believe that they were important; as if this were something he wanted desperately. Dawlish began to understand a little; Orde *wanted* everything he could get—and when a man wanted a thing badly enough, it was easier to make him believe that he had it.

'Well, hurry,' Dawlish said dryly. 'The police are still after Vanessa and me.'

'You'll be all right here,' Orde said. 'Where's Benoni?'

Now part of what Dawlish had planned and said was recoiling on his own head. He had said there was a time-limit for Benoni in the cave; that the police would hear about him unless he were released by the following evening. Now Orde wanted two or three days' grace, and there was nothing unreasonable about that. But if he told where Benoni was, he was giving away one of the tricks in his hand.

He hadn't long to make up his mind.

He said abruptly, 'Benoni's in a cave by a river called the Moro.' He went to the Esso map, indicated the spot and gave it to Orde.

Orde said, 'He'd better be there.'

He turned on his heel and went out; but in a moment he was back.

'You can go where you like on foot, Dawlish, but you can't drive away, and if you take advice you'll stay near the camp. You needn't worry about Vanessa, she'll be all right. Alice will be around to look after you.'

'Where are you going?' Dawlish demanded.

Orde said, 'I'm going to check these.' He raised his clenched hands, with the little rolls of paper in them. 'They'd better be right.'

He went out.

The doors clanged behind him. Silence fell, but before long the engine of a car started up. Dawlish was sure that Orde was leaving the camp.

The sound of the engine died away.

Now he had to wait. He had brought the tracings from London when he had fled, because he had believed all along that he must first find the man who had branded him, then win his confidence. They were genuine, and that could be proved.

This period of waiting was going to be worse than any he had known.

There was 'Alice' to help pass the time away.

There was Vanessa.

There were doubts and fears—and the knowledge that Orde was going to check the tracings with experts; that Orde was even now on his way to consult with—whom?

His scientific expert, obviously.

Who was he? What did he do?

Now that the situation was created other things emerged. Orde was a buyer in a big way, a man M.I.5 and the American Secret Service would want desperately. Did he work for himself or for others?

Finding that out really mattered *most*.

Clearing himself had seemed all-important, but it wasn't Revealing Orde for what he was, and finding his principals— they became the vital things.

Dawlish lit another cigarette. Now he knew what he had to try to do first, and could forget himself in the greater cause.

He went out for a walk, feeling strangely calm, and saw no one—except the dark shapes of the dogs. The fire had died away to embers, and no men sat round it. He might have been entirely on his own. He went back to the shack—and found that while he had been away, someone had pulled a bed down from the wall; there it was, with a comfortable interior sprung mattress, everything he could want—and the unspoken advice: Go to bed. . . .

He must not do anything to quicken Orde's doubts; must be patient.

He undressed. His case had been brought in, and his pyjamas and everything he wanted were handy. There was a hand-basin fed with water from a tank which he couldn't see.

He dozed for a while, then dropped off.

Suddenly, the door opened.

Dawlish lay sleeping. There was hardly a sound but the creaking as the door widened; the outer door and then the mesh frame. Both closed; softly, with hardly a sound.

A floor-board creaked.

Dawlish woke. On the instant, he knew that someone was in the room; he felt his heart leap wildly, and his body stiffened; but he did not move; he was trying to see who it was. He heard a rustling of movements, a soft breathing.

Then:

'Pat,' Vanessa said in a whisper. 'Pat, wake up.'

CHAPTER XX

BIG CHANCE?

'Pat,' repeated Vanessa, 'wake up.'

'What the hell are you doing here?'

'*Listen.*' Her hand groped and found his; she squeezed. 'We can get away. I've killed the dogs.'

That came so quickly, smoothly, convincingly. '*We can get away. I've killed the dogs*' He heard her gasping breath, as if she were terrified; and as if she had just come through some great physical exertion. 'There are only two guards, and one of them's—' She paused.

'Yes?'

'Dead.'

'How—'

'He got fresh,' she said. 'He just got fresh! He didn't know what was coming to him.'

Yes, that was Vanessa speaking; that was the woman who had a killer instinct which was always near the surface.

'The girl—' she began, and stopped.

Dawlish struggled up to a sitting position. Suddenly, he wanted to wring Vanessa's neck. Suddenly, he was afraid that she had killed Alice. He wanted to shout the question at her, but forced himself to say nothing; to wait.

'She's locked in her shack,' Vanessa said. 'There's just the one guard left, and he won't cause you any trouble. There's an alarm wire running round the camp but you can clear that.'

Dawlish was getting out of bed.

'How did you do all this?'

'I told you, one of the guards got fresh,' she said in a tense whisper. 'Don't waste time asking questions; get up, get dressed, *hurry!*'

She had forgotten a lot of things apparently; she had forgotten that he had wanted to come here, that there was no reason why he should want to get away so soon. He wished he could see her clearly. He groped for his clothes, pulled on his trousers, his shoes and a shirt, and then went with her towards the door.

Just outside, in the pale light of the stars, was the body of one of the dogs. Not far away was the body of the second. They were still warm, but lay stretched out on their sides and there could be no doubt that they were dead. Dawlish wondered how she had managed to kill them—and then thrust the thought out of his mind.

'This way,' she said.

'Where's the dead guard?'

'Don't waste time! There's a car over here, we can get away.'

'I want to see the dead guard,' Dawlish said.

'Are you *crazy?*' She spat the words at him, but changed her direction. The dead guard was near the fire. There were only a few embers glowing now, and the light came from the heavens. There was a strange silence about them; a hush, as of death. The man lay on the ground, crumpled up, his face towards the stars. Dawlish knelt down beside him. There was a knife in his back; a knife with a small handle, and buried to the hilt. He could believe what had happened; that she had let him kiss her, hug her, maul her—and then stabbed him to death.

Vanessa—the killer.

'Hurry,' she breathed.

'You've made a lot of mistakes, Vanessa,' Dawlish said. 'I've got business with Orde. I'm staying here. So are you.'

She didn't speak, but one moment she was touching him, the next she had turned. She ran towards the path which he could just see, a dark, flying figure. He could make out her shape. He stood watching, tight-lipped, hard-eyed. She hadn't gone fifty yards before a sudden beam of light shot out. A torch beam shone on to Vanessa; then another, then another. The trees were suddenly alive with men.

Dawlish turned back towards his shack. No one took any notice of him. He heard Vanessa scream; that was all. He kept imagining that he could feel the handle of the knife which she had buried in a man's back. He saw the dogs again, dark, stiff shapes. He felt sick. He had known from the beginning that he would meet unmentionable horrors in this affair, but he had not thought it possible that he would meet a woman like Vanessa.

Heartless—ruthless—cruel.

Yet beneath all that, a quality he could not hate.

He tried to put the words and the thoughts out of his mind, but they would not go. He switched on the light of the shack. It was just as he had left it. He kept tormenting himself about Vanessa. Then he found himself wondering whether Alice was all right, or whether some sixth sense had warned Vanessa not to say that she had killed the other woman.

He wanted to know the truth.

He didn't undress again, but laid down at full length, and tried to doze; but his mind seethed.

* * *

'Hi,' Alice said.

She wore the same clothes, looked fresh and sweet, and smiled across at him from the door. Dawlish had washed and shaved, and was drying his face.

'You want some coffee?' Alice asked.

'It sounds a good idea.'

'Sleep well?' She had a coffee percolator in her hand and put it on the hot-plate, which she switched on.

'No,' he said. 'I was disturbed.'

She said, 'I know what you mean.' She frowned and closed her eyes as if to shut out a vision. 'I don't know what made her do it. I can't imagine what made her think that she had a chance to get away. *You* knew better than that.'

'There's a difference,' Dawlish said. 'She didn't have any reason to want to stay. I'm waiting for a million dollars. Has Orde sent for Benoni?'

'Yes, of course.' She brought him the coffee.

'Where is he now?'

'They'll take him to the *Silver Slipper*,' Alice said. 'You needn't worry about Benoni any more.' She sipped her own coffee, watching him all the time. 'If those documents you have given to Orde are false—'

Dawlish flared up at her.

'What's this talk about fake documents? What the hell do you think I came here for? I'm on the run and I need big money and a hide-out. That's it and all about it.' He hoped that his eyes looked as angry as his voice sounded. 'The quicker the better.'

She said more stiffly, 'Where are the other documents?'

'After this, Orde has to take some risks. He'll get them in exchange for a million dollars.' Dawlish lit a cigarette, finished his coffee and then gave a quick, harsh laugh. 'Not that I can be sure of trusting Orde. I'm crazy to take the chance, but I had to take a chance somewhere!'

'You can trust him,' Alice said. 'If he says a thing, he always means it.'

Dawlish didn't speak.

'You don't know Orde,' the girl went on. 'I don't suppose anyone will ever know him, really. They'll never know how he hated, how he *hates*, war. They'll never know what happened to him when his three sons were killed—two in the World War and one in Korea. I know a little—I was married to one of his sons,' she added, very simply. 'My father-in-law swore that he would find a way of stopping nations murdering each other. That's all war is, of course—we'd murder Russians and they'd murder us, if given the chance. It's happened down the ages and no governments have ever been able to stop it. Have they?'

Dawlish said very softly, 'No.'

'So he decided that if governments wouldn't, people must,' Alice said. 'He wasn't alone in thinking that. He soon made converts. Some of the wealthiest men in the United States, some of the richest men in the world, are with him. They finance him, and he buys up the secrets of war. He buys them and makes them, and soon he will be able to threaten governments with them. He always believed that there should be a kind of international police force, and—he's creating it. The only way to start was to have the secrets of all the weapons. You can understand that, can't you?'

Dawlish muttered, 'Yes.'

Not in his wildest moments had he thought that this might be the explanation—or one which Orde had made Alice believe. He had known of the megalomaniacs who had believed that they could succeed where governments had failed, he knew that they existed; in moments of bitterness he could sympathize with them. But in cold blood, *if* she were telling the truth, then a single man acting for a group of wealthy men was gathering together the secrets of nations; and would threaten to use them; and, because that was how things went, *might one day use them.*

If this were all true, then he understood what she had meant when talking of ideals.

'You could help him,' Alice said.

Dawlish said roughly: 'Oh no, I'm not crazy yet. I've got what he wants—and it will cost him a million dollars. If he wants to put the world right, that's fine, but he won't get any help from me.'

He saw her eyes frost over, as they had when he had talked like this once before. That didn't matter; what mattered was convincing her that he meant exactly what he said.

'So let's forget it,' Dawlish said. 'And let's get the cant out of our systems, too. He doesn't believe in mass murder but he doesn't mind murder one by one. Look at the killers he employs. Haffmeyer was murdered. He set out to kill me cold-bloodedly. He beat up Vanessa. He tried to terrorize me, using Kurt. He isn't much of an angel, Alice. He uses death to get what he wants. I've seen that kind of idealist before—what you really mean is, he's mad.'

She didn't speak.

Dawlish said roughly, 'And I'm hungry.'

'Listen,' Alice said, and didn't turn away from him. 'He's had to be ruthless. He sacrifices a few to save many.'

'So he's the arbiter between life and death? He's Justice itself? He's made himself God!' Dawlish almost snarled at her. 'He's fooled you and perhaps he's fooled the others, but he isn't fooling me. I want my million dollars and safety. And—I—want—my—breakfast.'

She turned on her heel.

He watched the doors close after her, wondering what was in her mind. It wouldn't be long before he had to make a final decision—about Orde and the girl. Did he know the truth now? Was he dealing with a man whose very mind had been turned by grief—who had become an almost maniacal believer in himself and his mission, to save mankind from war?

Had Alice told the truth when she had said that he had other, wealthy men supporting him? Was there a syndicate?

He went out, and walked about the camp. A dozen men were working, but the great saw was silent. No one took any particular notice of him. He saw the treble-strand wire fence round the camp and could believe that it was electrified at night; he didn't test it to find out if it were now. He saw a mound of freshly dug earth, and did not doubt that the two dogs had been buried there. Not far off was another; probably the grave of the man whom Vanessa had killed.

The day was fine; and warming up.

Dawlish had no idea how near to the highway he was; for all he could tell, he might be a hundred miles from civilization. Several cars were parked at one side of the camp, and although there was no guard, half a dozen men were within sight. Most of these carried guns in their belts. They looked like lumbermen, hefty, hardy, slow-moving. Now and again Dawlish heard sounds, as if axes were being used on trees a long way off.

He knew that wherever he went he was watched.

He came upon a shack—and suddenly, upon Kurt, at a corner.

The giant's arm was in plaster and a sling. He caught sight of Dawlish and drew back. His lips twisted over his teeth—those moist, red lips. The little eyes burned with a hatred which few things would satisfy. As Dawlish moved past him, he felt a great uneasiness; a certainty that Kurt would try to kill him if a chance came.

Dawlish shivered.

Above him, the great trees towered so that to see the tops

he had to crane his neck. They overawed him. He felt at once their majesty and a sense of their power. He wondered why Orde had chosen this place as a hide-out, whether there was any significance.

Then, suddenly, the calm of the morning was broken. Dawlish just heard a car, then saw it coming through the trees; it jolted to a standstill. Men ran towards it. The driver jumped out. Dawlish could hear his voice but not the words. Alice came hurrying from one of the shacks and the driver raced towards her.

Then they turned towards Dawlish.

They came swiftly; three men, each with a gun; and Alice. He could see the animation of her face, and the anxiety; and he could see the determination on the faces of the men. They might have been coming to kill. Other men were watching; it was clear that every man at the camp was suddenly on edge. A great fear that something had gone wrong, that the chance he had fought for had vanished, welled up in Dawlish's mind. He stood quite still, gritting his teeth, although he felt a desperate temptation to turn and run.

Alice called, 'We've got to hide you, the police are coming.'

So the police were nearly here.

They had been waiting, and were pouncing now that they thought Dawlish was at his journey's end.

CHAPTER XXI

HIDEAWAY

Dawlish didn't doubt all that; didn't doubt that the girl meant it when she said that they had to hide him. And he mustn't be caught, yet. It had been a vital job before; now the safety of nations might depend on learning all there was to know about Orde and his principals or his partners.

'This way,' Alice said quickly. 'George, you come with me, the others go and—'

The man named George was tall, thin, wiry. He took a revolver from his belt, an unspoken threat, or warning. With Alice between them, they hurried through the great trees, out of the bright sunlight of the camp towards the gloom of the groves; and as they went deeper among the trees, it seemed to grow darker. Soon, they turned off a path and were walking as Dawlish had once walked with Vanessa, over the uneven ground. Suddenly, George stopped.

'Okay,' he said.

He stood by the side of a tree which looked no greater than most of the others nearby. Just a tree. Dawlish stared at him.

George grinned. Dawlish didn't see him do anything, but part of the trunk of the tree moved—outward, as an opening door. There was no sound. There was just George's grin and Alice's eager manner. The 'door' was five feet high, opened by pressure on a root. Dawlish saw that it had been cunningly made; knew that unless it were examined closely, no one would see there was anything different from any other tree-trunk.

Inside, it looked black, just a void.

'There's food and water in there,' Alice said, 'you won't have to stay long, anyway.'

'We've got to hurry,' George said, and waved the gun. He obviously expected that Dawlish would put up a fight to keep outside. 'Get moving.'

'I think the police are after Vanessa,' Alice said. Her brown eyes glowed with anxiety. 'Hurry, Pat.'

So Dawlish had to go, although he did not know for certain what he was walking into; Alice might be betraying him, but—if they wanted to kill him, would they shut him up in here?

He went forward.

George watched, unblinking, gun in hand.

Dawlish ducked down to get inside. It was dark but it was roomy, too, he didn't touch the other side at first. He found that he could stand upright. He turned slowly, and the faint light from the forest came in. Outside, Alice stood looking—almost appealing.

'Keep quiet—we'll come as soon as it's safe.'

George gave a little sound that might have been a laugh; an ugly laugh. He said:

'You can't open it from the inside, son.'

The door began to close, and to shut the light out; shut Dawlish in. He stood, staring. Light gradually disappeared as the gap grew smaller. The last thing he saw was Alice's forearm, so smooth and golden-coloured; then he heard a click, and the door was closed. From outside, this looked like an ordinary tree.

There was a strong, earthy smell.

Dawlish stood rigid for fully five minutes, and then realized that it wasn't so dark as he had thought. Light filtered in through small holes which had been bored in the trunk. He went close to one of them and put his eye to it. He could see the forest; the great trees; even the shafts of sunlight a long way off. There were four or five holes, all about on a level with his chin—eye level to a man of average height.

He could see inside, too.

He did not know how great the tree was in circumference, but he could move round. There were seats, hewn in it. He found a cupboard, opened the door, saw the food and the drink which Alice had assured him were there—two thermos flasks, biscuits, chocolate. There were two electric torches and several spare batteries, too. For the first time since he had been shut in he felt an easing of his tension.

He could think beyond the hollow tree. . . .

Had the police traced Vanessa here? If so, how? Where was Vanessa now? Could they hide her, as they had hidden him? Was she anywhere to hide? Was she *dead*? What would happen if the police discovered those graves; he only guessed that they were graves, but what else could they be?

He sat quite still.

He heard the strange, small sounds of the forest: sounds which meant nothing to him, crackling, creeping, stealthy. He heard no footsteps, no sounds of footsteps. Now and again he looked through one of the spy-holes, but nothing changed.

He looked at his watch; the illuminated dial told him that it was eleven o'clock; he had been here for half an hour. Already, it seemed an age.

Then he heard sounds: sounds that might have been footsteps; then he heard voices. He stood up, keeping very still.

The door opened.

Dawlish heard a flurry of movement; saw shadowy shapes; saw a woman, coming in—*falling* in. Fear took a paralysing grip on him. He stretched out a hand to try to touch the door, but it was closing. The woman's body was in his way, he couldn't exert any pressure. He stepped over her, crouched, tried to put his shoulder to the door; he heard it as it closed.

Then a man *laughed* outside.

It was soft laughter; hissing laughter; a wheezing, alarming, diabolic sound. It came from very nearby. Dawlish could not identify the man, was only sure that it was a man. He didn't move. The laughter went on and on, and he knew that whoever it was wanted to terrify him, wanted to make him scream out, wanted him to lose his nerve.

He kept still.

'*Daw*lish,' a man said.

Dawlish didn't answer. Slowly he went down on one knee. He had the torch in his pocket. He took it out and shone it on the woman. It was Vanessa—pale-faced, with red scratches on her cheek and forehead, her hair a tangle of auburn, with leaves and mud in it. He switched the light off.

'*Dawlish*,' said the man outside. It was Orde.

Dawlish said, 'All right, what is it?'

'So you thought you could fool *me*. You couldn't fool me, no one could ever fool me,' Orde boasted. 'I wasn't fooled last night. And when I knew the police were moving in with the F.B.I. I *knew* what you'd done—you'd led them here.'

Well, in a way that was true.

Orde's voice, almost metallic and hardly real, was unmistakable now.

'I know what you were trying to do, Dawlish. You got closer than I thought anyone ever would, but not close enough.'

Dawlish didn't speak.

'Answer me!' Orde roared. 'You're after my secrets, trying to smash me; *you're* not a traitor.'

Dawlish said slowly, wearily: 'I'm on the run from folk at home, and you know what I can offer—and what price I want. Don't get any idea that you can get it for nothing.'

Orde gave that soft laugh again; a laugh which was worse than any threat.

'Still stubborn, Dawlish? I tell you, I *know*. Those papers you gave me—it was safe enough, wasn't it?—you gave me secrets that were stolen from Great Britain months ago. I have them already, it didn't prove a thing. Listen, Dawlish. You got close to me way back. You didn't realize it. I had to fix you—and you were fixed nicely, *perfectly*.' Orde broke off, as if for breath; was gloating, was almost sick with triumph. 'I paid Haffmeyer, he was good but not good enough. He would have talked. The F.B.I. were after him. I couldn't trust him, Dawlish, so what did I do? I waited until you were near his home, and killed him. I fixed him, fixed you—and now I've fixed Vanessa, the bitch! You'll both *burn*!'

The last word came out viciously. At first the meaning of it didn't really strike home. Dawlish was thinking of all that had gone before. Then he heard the words again: 'You'll burn.' Orde laughed, and it was the laughter which made Dawlish understand what he meant.

You'll burn.

'The police are on the way, and they might find the bodies, mightn't they? So I'm on my way out, Dawlish.' Then the laugh came out again, with its note of menace and its horror. 'There's only one way to hide all the traces, that's to *burn* the camp. We're starting. The wind is coming this way, a fine fresh wind.

Everything's tinder dry, so dry that it will burn fast, Dawlish, real fast. But you won't know much about it, after you've burned.'

Dawlish still didn't speak.

There were other sounds; he thought that they were footsteps, but wasn't sure. He expected Orde to call out again; the man didn't. He waited. He shone the torch on Vanessa again; she was unconscious. He felt her pulse; it was fairly steady. He sat her up against the side of the tree, and shone the torch into her eye. He saw that the pupil was a pin-point; she was drugged, probably with morphia.

Dawlish began to thrust his weight against the side of the tree, but there was no weak spot; no sign that any part of it would give way.

He shone the beam upwards.

The tree was hollowed out to a height of eight or nine feet, and the ceiling was conical in shape, and rough hewn. He did not think there was any chance of making a hole through the trunk without tools, and he had no knife. He looked in the store cupboard. There were plastic beakers, but no glass and no china, nothing that could make a kind of saw, or knife.

There was no way out.

He couldn't take a long step in any direction. He couldn't move without touching Vanessa. It was difficult to think about Vanessa—it was difficult to think about anything but that laughter, that metallic voice, and that threat: *You'll burn.*

Then Dawlish smelt smoke.

He put his eye to one of the spy-holes. Ahead of him were the other trees, massed in their great height; and here and there shafts of sunlight. Was it his imagination, or was there a smoky haze where the sun shone? Could it be mist or was it smoke from the fire?

It was *smoke.*

Dawlish turned slowly; his shoulders seemed to be wedged, because the woman on the floor restricted his freedom of movement. He looked out of one of the other holes—and saw flames.

They were not far off.

He saw them unmistakably, and there was much more smoke in that direction, billowing towards him. Here and there great white clouds of it hid the trees, then ran along the ground as if driven by a strong wind. The smell was overpowering.

The smoke itself seemed to light up; a great flame flashed in the middle of it, tinging the cloud, making it a turbulent, angry red. Next moment there was only a red glow everywhere. There were just the glow, the smoke, and the flames.

Dawlish could see these out of three of the spy-holes, and knew that the fire was creeping nearer.

He leaned against the trunk, his eyes closed.

Then he stirred himself, as smoke began to pour into the tree, making his eyes water, making them red and sore.

'Crazy fool!' he swore at himself. 'You don't deserve to live. Blithering idiot!' He tore pieces off his shirt and stuffed them into the holes to keep the smoke out. 'You won't *burn,* but you might suffocate.'

He began to cough.

Smoke filled the tree-trunk hollow, whirling about it. Dawlish couldn't stop coughing. He knew that he should have stuffed those holes before, that the greatest danger came from the smoke.

The paroxysm slackened off.

His eyes were sore, and his head began to ache. His chest ached, too. He couldn't breathe in clean air. He leaned against the hewn trunk, helpless—and nearer to hopelessness than he had ever been in his life. There wasn't a thing he could do.

He slid down the trunk, until he was sitting on the ground with his back against it—next to Vanessa.

His eyes were running; tears streamed down his cheeks, into his mouth. His breath was harsh, laboured, hurtful. He did not think that he would be able to stand it much longer—he would lose consciousness.

It was so hot.

The truth of that came to him slowly; as the truth about the smoke had done. It was unbearably hot. Not tears but sweat poured down his face, and broke out over his whole body; he was sitting in his own sweat.

Outside, the fire raged; outside, the tree was probably burning.

He couldn't really breathe.

It was so hot that he couldn't move without sweat pouring down him.

His head threatened to burst; and his chest threatened to burst. He resigned himself to death.

There was England. . . .

There was Felicity, his wife. . . .

His breathing grew more laboured still.

CHAPTER XXII

ALICE

The fire had started near the camp.

Orde came walking back through the forest towards the shacks. His men were moving some things into the cars, several of which were already on the way. The camp itself would be burned out of recognition. There was little chance that the police would make any further investigation here; and for days they would be too busy fighting the fire.

Alice watched Orde.

She saw him now as Dawlish saw him—pale-faced, with a strange feverish look in his eyes, with a quality which was hardly human. Bloodless. He looked like a robot; even his voice had an unreal, mechanical quality.

'Let's go,' he said, as he drew level with Alice.

'Where's Dawlish?' asked Alice.

'We'll pick him up later,' Orde said offhandedly.

'Where's the girl—Vanessa?'

'Forget her.'

'Dad—' began Alice.

'Forget her,' Orde said roughly. 'And forget Dawlish. He

fooled me, didn't I tell you? We haven't any time for Dawlish now.'

He grabbed her arm, and pulled her towards the cars. Already, smoke was blowing through the trees, and there was a tinge of red everywhere, earnest of the devouring fire which was to roar down upon this place. Alice went with Orde; there was no way she could break free, his fingers gripped her wrist so tightly.

George was at the wheel of a car.

'Hurry,' he said.

They got in. Orde continued to hold the girl's wrist until they were moving fast through the forest. The other cars had already gone ahead. The smoke was billowing behind them, already high in the heavens and dimming the bright sunlight where its shafts shone through the big trees. The car gathered speed, and Orde relaxed his grip.

There was a small dirt road some distance from the camp; and a few miles along that, a highway which would lead them to Highway 99. The cars, five in all, were spaced out, and no one could be sure that they were connected with one another.

Alice sat looking straight ahead of her.

She knew that there was an airfield, half an hour's journey away, where they would find an aeroplane waiting. She knew that all their traces at the camp would be burned away. She knew that Orde had built up an elaborate system, along Highways 99 and 101, and that he would not come back until he was sure that the police had not discovered what it was.

She knew, now, that Dawlish had made her understand the real truth—that Orde, sitting beside her and glaring in front of him, was mad. He was the father of the man she had loved, and she had known him as a good man, as one who placed his ideals above everything else; and for a long time she had been fooled, but she knew the truth now. He was mad; nothing would ever be safe with him.

If he were right and Dawlish had brought the police, then Dawlish had lied to her, and there was great goodness in the big man.

There were things Vanessa had said to her, also—bitter, burning things.

She knew that it would not be long before they reached the airfield. There was only one stretch of the county highway which would be dangerous: a few miles when they would have to merge with other traffic. Although the clouds of smoke were way behind them now, they would have been seen, the warning that there was a forest fire would have been sounded for miles around.

The police would want information from anyone coming from the forest.

So those few miles were dangerous. . . .

They reached the road, and George slowed down, so as to turn the corner. Two or three other cars were coming in the other direction, but there were no police in sight.

Alice had a hand on the door-handle.

Orde was staring in front of him.

Alice pressed the handle down and the door opened; wind cut in. George shouted. Orde grabbed at her as she leapt towards the open door. Orde's hand clutched at her skirt; for a moment she was half in and half out of the car. Then she wrenched herself free.

They were travelling at forty miles an hour.

She fell, hitting the ground with her shoulder first. Pain shot through her. She rolled over and over, and was flung clear of the wheels of the car, clear of the road. The pain was so great that she lost consciousness.

She didn't see Orde glaring at her out of the back window.

At the wheel, George shouted:

'What do we *do*?'

'Slow down,' Orde cried. 'Slow down!' That was a waste of words, George had already slowed down. Orde took a gun from his pocket, opened the window and leaned out. The girl was fifty yards off now, lying quite still. There was blood on the road. He fired at her three times. He couldn't be sure that any of the bullets struck her body; but he didn't see them kick up dirt in the road.

He dropped back into the car.

'Step on it,' he ordered savagely. 'Step on it.'

Cars were passing on the other side.

Drivers and passengers saw the crumpled figure.

'That's right,' a policeman said, 'she fell out of a car. That's the story.' He didn't look away from the crushed figure of the girl. She lay on the side of the road, where passing motorists had carried her. Her body was twisted badly, her head and one side of her face were bloody; no one who saw her thought that she had a chance to live.

The siren of an ambulance sounded.

The girl's eyes flickered. None watching her had dreamed that there was any hope that she would ever come round again; but there was no doubt that her eyes flickered. She looked about her dazedly. Her lips moved. The policeman, a youngster with a fresh-coloured face and ginger hair, went down on one knee.

'You want to say something, honey?'

She looked desperately into his face.

'Hollow tree,' she said. 'Two—people. Hollow tree. Two people. Get them—out.'

Her eyes closed.

'You hear that?' said a man close by, as the ambulance came screeching up. 'She said there's two people in a hollow tree. Gee—and that forest's on fire!'

'How'd she *know*?' a man asked, pointlessly.

Dawlish knew that he was alive.

He had lost consciousness but had come round; but that was as far as he had got yet. He had been near death and was alive. He was still hot—unbearably hot, and sticky. Breathing was difficult, and his chest hurt, and there was the smell of burning. But he was alive.

There was a weight against his shoulder; Vanessa, of course. Orde had said something about Vanessa, but Dawlish couldn't remember what it was. Orde must have been gone for some time.

He—was—alive.

He began to think more clearly, and knew that there was little reason to hope. He couldn't get out. He was physically done, and even with his full strength he had been unable to get free, so this was the end. The fire might have passed them by, with no worse that a severe scorching, but he still hadn't a chance. There was no way out. There was the drink and the chocolate, but they wouldn't last long. There was no way of attracting attention; no cause to hope.

He shifted his position.

He had no idea how long he had been here. It was pitch dark, but that might be because of the holes which he had bunged up. He struggled to his feet, and Vanessa fell sideways; he thought he heard her catch her breath. Never mind Vanessa. He unplugged one of the holes and put his eye to it.

He could see *sunlight*. There was a haze of smoke, too, but not billowing and not red-tinged. He felt sure that the worst of the fire was past. He could not understand how it was that they had come to live through it, unless it was because he had stuffed up the spy-holes.

He opened the cupboard, unstoppered a thermos, poured a little water unsteadily into a beaker, and then put that on a shelf, to steady himself. He took a sip. Then he went down on one knee, straightened Vanessa, and put the beaker to her lips.

She sipped and coughed.

There was food and more drink.

They could live for *days. . . .*

But supposing they did? They would die eventually; he had to remind himself that there wasn't a way out.

Crazy! There *must* be! He hadn't even tried. What was the matter with him—with him, Patrick called Pat Dawlish? He was as strong as a horse wasn't he? He could break the arm of a man like Kurt, couldn't he? All right, break down the tree; there was a door, and that meant there was weakness at the trunk. What the hell did he mean by giving up?

He flung himself against the inside wall, brushing his shoulders, shaking his body. He made no impression at all. He drew back, sweat pouring down his body, soaking his clothes.

Vanessa spoke in a croaking voice.

'Where—where are we?'

'We—we'll be all right,' Dawlish said. 'Don't worry. We'll be all right.'

There was silence; then, 'Where—are—we?' Vanessa asked, as if he hadn't spoken.

She was nearly delirious.

He gave her a little more to drink and tried to reason with her, but he knew that he would get no sense out of her. She talked foolishly, stupidly. Now and again as he bent over her she struck at him. Sometimes she giggled. It seemed to get hotter, and the harsh smell of burning and of smoke made them cough—sometimes in unison, as if they would never be able to stop.

Then, suddenly, Dawlish heard a different sound.

He was coughing; yet the sound came through, as of a man's voice. Vanessa was coughing, and he wanted to strike her, to do anything to make her stop; he desperately wanted silence.

Yes, there were voices.

He held his breath, and Vanessa stopped unexpectedly; inside the tree there was silence, but outside there were sounds of men walking; of heavy footsteps; and of men calling.

Dawlish began to shout, to bellow, to kick against the side of the tree—and then his exertions got too much for him, and he started to cough. He felt as if he would never be able to stop; but the paroxysm passed.

Then a man called: 'Jim, they're here! Sheriff, thisaway!'

CHAPTER XXIII

THE PRINCIPALS

Dawlish felt the coolness of the evening air on his face; the nectar of air which was not laden with smoke. He was sitting by the side of a clearing, where the fire had not penetrated. Police were moving about. There were several cars. Vanessa was in one of these; she had come round, and was still rather stupid—giggling stupid.

One of the men came up to Dawlish—Sheriff Delano, he knew. He was tall, dark-haired, and needed a shave; to look at, he might have been one of the lumbermen.

'You feel more yourself?'

'Sure.'

'That's fine. You haven't told me your name yet, stranger.' The Sheriff's eyes seemed to be full of accusation. 'Nor the lady's, but I guess she's Mrs. Haffmeyer. Mrs. *Vanessa* Haffmeyer. You know what she's wanted for?'

Dawlish found himself grinning.

'That's right,' he said. 'And I'm Dawlish and I know what I'm wanted for, too. But Haffmeyer's real killers locked us up in that tree.' He didn't need to labour that point; he had only one thing

197

to do that really mattered. 'Sheriff, I want to send a message to a certain Leonard Massala; you'll find him in San Francisco. He's F.B.I.' Massala was a man with whom Dawlish had worked, months ago. A safe man. 'It's so urgent you can't get word to him quick enough. Tell him that Dawlish wants him, and tell him that a big shot was at the camp here. Also—'

He talked for two minutes.

The Sheriff did not ask for anything to be repeated, but went off, to use the radio-telephone in his car. Dawlish felt desperately anxious to see Massala.

Massala was small, dark, a bundle of live wires. He was at the little forest town within three hours. By then, Dawlish knew how the police had been told about him and Vanessa; and knew also that Alice had died before she had got to hospital. He knew, too, that nothing was likely to be found at the camp—although, at his suggestion, some digging through the hot earth had been done; police had found the bodies of the dogs and of the man whom Vanessa had killed.

'So you found this Orde and drove him away—what else did you find out?' asked Massala.

Dawlish said, 'Only the girl's story.' He didn't know what Massala felt about the tale that Orde was an idealist gone wrong. Massala wouldn't refuse to believe it simply because he hadn't any proof.

'Could be,' Massala said. He smoothed down his wiry hair, and his teeth flashed. 'You've had a bad time, I guess, but there are some facts, Dawlish. We have to know whom Orde works for. Maybe it isn't Russia! Maybe it's for a syndicate of crazy guys, but we need to know who those guys are. You haven't found that out, and you were the man with a chance to find out. Remember?'

Dawlish said: 'Orde had to get in touch with his backers—this syndicate—regularly. They would be on this side of the country, or he wouldn't have made his headquarters here. I'd say that he had to have meetings, conferences, and consultations—and I'd guess that those principals aren't so far away.'

Massala looked sceptical, half smiling, as if expecting a statement much more factual than that.

Dawlish smiled faintly, 'It's guesswork, and I can imagine how you feel.'

'I can imagine how *you* feel. You've done everything except find out the final thing, maybe the one thing that could start it all over again. We have to know who Orde worked with. Maybe Vanessa Haffmeyer can help.' Massala stood up and began to walk restlessly about the room where the others had left them. 'Did Vanessa kill her husband or didn't she? We've got to find out, Dawlish. We can hold that murder over her and make her talk about the rest, I guess.'

Dawlish kept a poker face. 'I think I know where we can get a lead on Orde's principals without trying to make Vanessa talk by using threats,' he said.

Massala didn't speak; just waited.

'Have you ever seen one of the publicity sheets offered by the various restaurant and hotel chains?' Dawlish asked.

Massala looked blank.

'Here's one,' Dawlish said. He took out a folded serviette, which he had taken from the *Silver Slipper*. On it was marked most of the towns and villages on the Redwood Highway; and also marked were a dozen or more restaurants, including the *Silver Slipper*, the *Golden Shoe* and the *Shoestring*. There was the *Long Stocking* and the *Shake a Leg*, the *Jackboot*, the *Shoe Tree*. Every restaurant in the chain had some association with foot-wear or stockings.

Massala read the plan and looked up. His eyes began to glow.

'So what?'

'Benoni, manager of the *Silver Slipper,* really mattered to Orde,' Dawlish said dryly. 'He was so important that Orde took a lot of risks for him, and made it clear he wanted Benoni safe. It wouldn't be because of Benoni's bright eyes—but because of the job he did. He'd be high up—and he was a restaurant manager. I think we'll find that all of these restaurants are used in the business, Massala. We'll find these are the places where the principals meet. Pick up all the managers, they're probably highly placed in the organization, and in Orde's pocket. If you can't crack them, you can start on Vanessa.'

Massala was already on his feet.

Dawlish felt tired.

He had not yet heard from Massala, but believed it wouldn't be long before they knew who bought and sold secrets which could affect the lives of millions. He would soon know his own fate, too.

He had sent a cable to Felicity, but hadn't had an answer. He longed hungrily to see his wife. He wanted to talk over their own fireside, to explain how he had missed her. He wanted to tell her what he thought about Alice, who had given her life to save him once she realized the truth about Orde.

He wanted to tell his wife about Vanessa.

He wanted *rest.*

But there were still things to do; or there was one thing to do.

Vanessa was in the nearest hospital. He would be told when she was conscious again—and when her mind was clear. He didn't like thinking about her.

The telephone bell rang.

He answered it as he heard Sheriff Delano come into the room. He looked up at the Sheriff and winked.

It was the hospital. Vanessa was awake, level-headed, and asking for Dawlish. He said he would go, and then looked up at the Sheriff, who shrugged and smiled faintly.

'Sure—I'll drive you myself,' he said.

The hospital was a single-storey building with a lot of glass windows, and no formality. A young intern was with Vanessa when Dawlish reached the private room where she lay in bed. The Sheriff didn't come in, but waited out in the passage, his ten-gallon hat in his hand.

Vanessa looked—beautiful.

There were the scratches, but they hardly spoiled her. Her eyes were at their glowing best. She smiled as she stretched out a hand to Dawlish. Her fingers were cool. She pulled him down and kissed him, and then let him go and looked at him as if at her beloved.

'Hallo—Pat for Patrick!'

'Hi, Vanessa.'

'You're doing fine with the language.' But that wasn't what she meant to say. Her eyes had an almost hungry, longing look. 'Pat, you *are* alive. That's so hard to believe. I was sure that Orde would kill you. He came very close. You ought to have taken my advice, and run away before, Pat. I had the money.'

'I know what you mean,' Dawlish said, 'but I had another job to do. Remember?'

'I remember,' Vanessa said. 'And you did it, with a lot more. You weren't seduced from duty by your Vanessa, were you?' Her eyes showed a kind of hurt laughter. 'Pat, do you want a big shock?'

'Try me,' he said.

'I'll do just that. I was waiting for *you*, Pat for Patrick Dawlish, at my house that night. I'd been told you were on the way. I expected you to make a deal with Gurth Haffmeyer. I knew he was selling out on big government secrets, and I'd been told you were the buyer.'

She paused.

Dawlish began to smile, very gently. And his heart leapt with great hope.

Vanessa went on:

'So I waited for you, but he was killed first. I don't know who killed him—for all I knew, you had. I sent for help—for Kell. That's why the F.B.I. man came. But I just had to check on you, I had to find out which side you were really on. That was my job, Pat. When you showed up, it might have been your second visit—you might have killed Gurth, gone away and come back. I had to be sure what you were, so I just strung along. I did all I could to make you show how bad you were. Patrick!' There was the laughter of pain in her eyes. 'I began to realize you were mostly good, a long way back. But I didn't know Orde, only as a name. I wanted to find him, too. And my boss told me to keep close to you, whatever else I did. Like to know who my boss is?'

Dawlish said mildly, 'Name of Uncle Sam?'

'That's right,' Vanessa said. 'The great American Secret Service, Pat! And I hope I fooled you plenty—but I was never quite sure. Did I?'

'You did at first,' Dawlish said. 'But I soon realized that the police weren't exerting themselves to find us, so I guessed they had us tailed. That's when I began to wonder about you. Vanessa—that killer streak in you—'

'I killed that red shirt driver because it was the only way to save you—to save the two of us. And I showed a killer streak because I wanted you to think I was as bad as they came,'

Vanessa said. 'That way, you'd be more likely to tell me the truth if Haffmeyer had lied about you.'

Dawlish said, 'He lied.'

'Why didn't anyone tell you?' asked Vanessa, as if astounded. 'I had a telephone message only just now. Orde and some of his men have been caught and held. One man talked, and you're in the clear. In fact we're both in the clear, because the man who shot my husband has confessed. Orde knew you were going to see Gurth; it was quite a frame-up. It's lucky I was there!'

He knew that she wasn't lying, and his heart and mind had gone serenely quiet. He sensed, too, that she felt the same deep satisfaction of relief.

It wasn't long before Massala telephoned to the Sheriff's office confirming the news. The first of the restaurant managers had cracked.

There had been regular conferences at the *Shoestring*. Orde had attended them all; Haffmeyer had been to one or two. The first names of the syndicate members—names which obviously meant a lot to Massala, but little to Dawlish—had come from the restaurant manager who had cracked.

As the days passed more and more names came in. Dawlish learned how widespread it had been; world-wide. Americans, Canadians, South Americans, Indians, Japanese—people of all nationalities, men of great wealth, had banded together to rob governments of secrets which, if betrayed to the wrong powers, might decimate millions of people. There may have been idealism at the beginning; there may have been the dream of ending war. But this syndicate had started to feel its own power—its corrupting power of controlling the destinies of nations.

The story began to reach the headlines. . . .

Dawlish went to see Vanessa one day to talk about the latest names, but found her gone from her hotel. He was astonished—until he read the note which she had left for him.

I can tell when I've lost, Pat, she had written. *You never stop thinking about your wife, do you? Say 'Hi,' to her, from me.*

Vanessa.

Dawlish flew to Washington, and talked; flew to New York, and talked; and then flew to London, where he would have to talk again. It was strange to be able to travel without the feeling that anyone was on his trail; strange to feel that he could trust everyone he spoke to; strange to feel that there was no danger from a knife or bullet. Stranger, wonderful, to know that all men trusted him.

Felicity was waiting for him in London.

He could forget Alice, almost forget Vanessa, forget the horrors that had been and might have been, forget the smoky hole of torment in the big tree, whenever he thought of Felicity.

For there was goodness in her, and peacefulness, all the things he needed.

ABOUT THE AUTHOR

John Creasey, born in 1908, was a paramount English crime and science fiction writer who used myriad pseudonyms for more than six hundred novels. He founded the UK Crime Writers' Association in 1953. In 1962, his book *Gideon's Fire* received the Edgar Award for Best Novel from the Mystery Writers of America. Many of the characters featured in Creasey's titles became popular, including George Gideon of Scotland Yard, who was the basis for a subsequent television series and film. Creasey died in Salisbury, UK, in 1973.

THE PATRICK DAWLISH MYSTERIES

FROM OPEN ROAD MEDIA

INTEGRATED MEDIA

Find a full list of our authors and
titles at www.openroadmedia.com

FOLLOW US
@OpenRoadMedia